**I had been summoned home from the asylum, and given a chance to prove once and for all that I did not kill my mother. My journey of redemption did not bode well for the real killer, who watched from the shadows, waiting...**

A knot formed in my stomach. It started out as fear, but blossomed into rage when I saw the knife embedded in the tree not three inches from where I had just been leaning. Had I not moved, it would have landed in my neck. Now it was wedged up to its hilt in the trunk of the tree that I had leaned against.

Grabbing the slick, colorful handle, I wrenched the embedded knife out of the tree and studied it. It was exactly like the one I had found in my father's desk drawer, like the knife that had killed Gran. Bright stripes of yellow, red, purple, and green decorated the handle. I ran my finger along the shiny steel blade. It sliced through my skin. A tiny trickle of my blood seeped out of the small wound.

I took the handkerchief that I had used to wipe my mouth and wrapped the knife in it then tucked the bundle in my pocket. I applied pressure to the small cut I had made, until it stopped bleeding. Then I continued on the path toward safety, moving as quickly as I could without tumbling. Vivian Mason had just tried to kill...

Sarah Bennett doesn't remember the night her mother tumbled down the stairs at Bennett House, despite allegedly witnessing the fatal fall. There was talk of foul play, dark whispers, and sidelong glances, all aimed at Sarah, prompting her family to send her to The Laurels, an exclusive asylum in San Francisco, under a cloud of suspicion.

Now, on the one-year anniversary of her mother's murder, Sarah has been summoned home. Convinced of her innocence, she returns to Bennett House, hoping to put the broken pieces of her life back together. But when another murder occurs shortly after her arrival, Sarah once again finds herself a suspect, as she is drawn into a web of suspicion and lies.

In order to clear her name, Sarah must remember what happened the fateful night her mother died. But as she works to regain her memory, the real murderer watches, ready to kill again to protect a dark family secret.

# KUDOS for *The Spirit of Grace*

In *The Spirit of Grace* by Terry Lynn Thomas, Sarah Bennett has just come home from an asylum where she was sent after her mother, Jessica Bennett, died from a fall down the stairs. Although Sarah was found at the base of the stairs, cradling her dead mother in her arms, she can't remember what happened that night. So everyone thinks that she murdered her mother. A year later, in 1942, Sarah is summoned home by her father and she returns to Bennett House, in the small town of Bennett's Cove, just north of San Francisco. When she gets there, she finds to her dismay that her father has published a book, remarried, and taken on an assistant, Zeke, whom Sarah suspects is a spy. As the tension mounts in the household, Sarah struggles to remember what happened the night her mother died, while trying to fight her growing feelings for Zeke, and her growing animosity for her young stepmother, who is about the same age as Sarah. The story has a strong plot, filled with many twists and turns, and takes you back to the time of the World War II, when anyone who was a stranger was suspected of being a spy. The author's voice is fresh and unique and the story will grab your interest from the very first page. ~ *Taylor Jones, Reviewer*

*The Spirit of Grace* by Terry Lynn Thomas is a World War II drama, rife with murder, spies, suspense, deceit, betrayal, and page-turning excitement. Our heroine, Sarah, has temporary amnesia about the night her mother died. Suspected of pushing her mother down the stairs to her death, Sarah leaves her home in Bennett Cove, California, under a cloud of suspicion, and spends a year in an asylum, in hopes her memory will return. Our story opens in October 1942, when Sarah has been called home by her father after a year of being away at the asylum. When she arrives at her home, Bennett House, she discovers that her father has remarried a woman named Grace, who is nearly the same age as Sarah. Although she tries to like the woman and wants her father to be happy, Sarah feels an immediate animosity toward Grace. She also feels an immediate attraction to Zeke, her father's new assistant. But this is a time of war, and people are not what they seem. When another murder occurs, Sarah is the prime suspect, but this time her memory is unaffected and she knows she is innocent. Now she just has to *clear her name. If she lives that long. The* Spirit of Grace is a combination mystery/thriller of the first order. Thomas has done an excellent job of both crafting a believable world in the middle of World War II and creating realistic and endearing characters. This one will catch your interest from the very first word and hold it straight through to the end. ~ *Regan Murphy, Reviewer*

# ACKNOWLEDGEMENTS

*The Spirit of Grace* was a long time in the making, from idea to final publication. Many hands touched this book, each making it better in the process. Humble gratitude to my beta readers, Diane Greer and Lynn Petersen, whose expertise in the ways of the human mind helped me to make my characters deeper. Lara Long, Stanly Brown, John Harper, Diane Godwin, and Elizabeth Thomas, your feedback helped so much, your support and encouragement kept me going.

A heartfelt thanks to Lauri Wellington, acquisitions editor at Black Opal Books, for giving *The Spirit of Grace* a home and to the editors at Black Opal Books who helped polish this book to perfection.

My fabulous critique partner, Lisa Ricard Claro, whose editing and storytelling expertise never ceases to amaze. Lisa, thanks for being there through the laughter, the tears, and the emergency plotting issues and character crises. How lucky I was to find you at a writing conference so long ago!

And, finally, thanks and love to my husband, Doug, who believed in me from the beginning.

# THE
# SPIRIT
# OF
# GRACE

TERRY LYNN THOMAS

*A Black Opal Books Publication*

GENRE: HISTORICAL MYSTERY/PARANORMAL THRILLER/RO-
MANTIC ELEMENTS/SUSPENSE

THE SPIRIT OF GRACE
Print ISBN: 978-1-626943-96-4

First Publication: JANUARY 2016

Published by Black Opal Books **http://www.blackopalbooks.com**

*In loving memory of Dorothy Kelly Fenstermaker.*

# CHAPTER 1

*San Francisco, October 1942*:

The sun shone the day I left the asylum. I fled the protection of the big house on the hill, with its magnificent view of the Pacific Ocean, its competent nurses, and mind-numbing routine, and entered a world at war and a city preparing for invasion. When Gran and my father had swept me away to The Laurels, the war that raged in Europe was a distant threat. When I got out of the taxi cab on Van Ness Avenue in front of Zim's—hatless, gloveless, and dressed in the street clothes that I hadn't worn in a very long time—reminders of America's entry into the war were everywhere, from the staccato bulletins read non-stop over radios that blared out of the shops on Van Ness Avenue, to the glaring headlines pronouncing the grim facts of the fighting.

My trek along the short block to the front door of the restaurant resembled a running of the gauntlet. With my valise in tow, I wove between throngs of uniformed soldiers who spilled out of the entrances of shops, restaurants, and bars. When I finally wrestled my way to the hostess at Zim's, I was out of breath and sweating, despite the chilly San Francisco air.

"Miss Bennett," she said, "It's been a long time." When she realized why she hadn't seen me—information she had gleaned from the newspaper headlines—she stammered. "I'm sorry—I didn't realize—"

"It's okay, really." I smiled at her. "I've been craving a burger for a while."

She nodded and beckoned me to follow her to a secluded table in the back of the restaurant.

"Do you have a newspaper?"

"Of course," she said. She soon came back with a *San Francisco Chronicle* and a *New York Times*. When the waitress came, I ordered the Zim's burger with extra fries and a strawberry shake without looking at the menu.

"We're out of hamburger meat," the waitress said.

"What? I don't understand."

"Meat shortage. We just sold out for the day. Sorry." She looked around at her other tables as she tapped her pencil on her order pad.

"Just the fries and shake."

She nodded and hurried away, stopping to flirt with a table of soldiers who were seated in the booth next to mine.

While I ate, I read about the relentless aerial bombing in England. My heart broke as I read about the children who were being sent to the countryside to live with strangers, while their parents stayed in the city, to face those bombs alone. This war had wound its tentacles around everyone. We were a nation united in the pursuit of a single enemy. We were encouraged to grow our victory gardens, donate all scrap metal, and keep our mouths shut. "Loose lips sink ships" was the catch phrase plastered on billboards and written on posters that were taped to telephone poles and hung in shop windows.

California was home to more than its share of air bases, naval bases, naval shipyards, and repair facilities, but I was surprised that so many soldiers were queued up for the bus ride to Bennett Cove, a small town nestled just north of San Francisco—on the other side of a breathtaking mountain with trails winding through lush ferns—abutting the Pacific Ocean. Our coastline boasted riptides and black seals whose heads bobbed just off shore in the evening, staring at the beachgoers with sweet faces that resembled those of devoted dogs.

The only other female passenger on the bus was Mrs. Tolliver, Bennett Cove's resident witch. Lovelorn women visited her in secret, careful to stay unseen by friends and neighbors, as they navigated the footpath concealed in the

redwoods that led to Mrs. Tolliver's cottage. She would
tell their fortunes in exchange for food, hand-me-down
clothes, and the occasional coin. When Mrs. Tolliver
fixed her attention upon you, her gaze penetrated right
through to the soulful spot where the secret truths lay
hidden.

I opened my newspaper and stared at it, hoping that
she wouldn't see me. No such luck.

"Sarah Bennett," she cried out. "I'm so pleased that
you've come home." She wriggled her ample hips, as she
squeezed into the seat next to me. "Your father must have
summoned you?"

I opened my mouth to say yes, but Mrs. Tolliver continued to speak.

"He's a saint, that man. He paid off the bank note on
my house after the husband passed. He would have paid
for electricity too, but I don't believe in electricity. No.
The vapors will make a body sick."

She scrutinized me, head to toe, judging me like a
piece of meat at the butcher's. She carried a burlap shopping bag with leather handles worn slick by decades of
use. Now she placed it on the floor underneath her seat,
careful with its breakable contents. She smelled of garlic
and sweat and the homemade lye soap she used to wash
her clothes. She wore her long gray hair in a bun, revealing thick dark streaks of grit and dirt along the back of
her sun-burnt neck. She smelled as though she hadn't had
her bath this week.

I wondered if I could crack my window without giving offense.

"Anyone worth their salt knows you didn't kill your mother," she said. "You haven't got the stomach for it. It's been one year, today, hasn't it?"

Unable to speak, I nodded. I didn't remember anything of the night my mother fell down the stairs at Bennett House and broke her neck. My father and grandmother had found me huddled over my mother's body, shivering in my nightgown, and mumbling incoherently. They thought I had killed her. Everyone in Bennett Cove thought I pushed her down the stairs to her death. I didn't know one way or another. I didn't remember a thing about that night.

The psychiatrist, whom my father hired to care for me, diagnosed chronic amnesia and had suggested I stay at his asylum for a rest, in hopes that my memory would come back. I had done my part, participated in the tests and therapy groups, but my memory hadn't returned. That part of my life, the time when my mother died, was a yawing chasm in my psyche.

Out of the blue, my father had summoned me home. The time had come for me to try to remember what happened the night my mother died, to exonerate the cloud of suspicion that hung over my head. The time had come for me to slay my demons.

Mrs. Tolliver jabbed my ribs with her elbow. "You listening?" She looked at me with squinty eyes.

I smiled at her. "Are all these soldiers going to Bennett Cove?"

"That they are," she said. "Bennett Cove is billeting troops before they ship out. There's no room for them in the city, so they've set up an encampment. The place is swarming with soldiers. A body can hardly get to the post office anymore, I tell you, and I'll be glad when this war is over. I only hope that we don't get invaded." Mrs. Tolliver pushed her sweater aside to show a gun holstered underneath the waistband of her skirt.

I gasped.

"Don't look so surprised. Things aren't what they used to be. A body's got to be protected."

The bus drove down Lombard Street and soon passed a billboard depicting a larger than life-size picture of my father, holding his book, *The Arms of the Enemy*. He grinned, the smile of a man who hadn't a care in the world.

"Have you read his book yet?" Mrs. Tolliver asked.

"No," I said. "They didn't allow books involving crime at—where I stayed."

"It's very good," Mrs. Tolliver said. "Elegant writing for a man. And don't look at me with surprise. Just because I'm simple doesn't mean I'm stupid. I read all the time." She leaned back and crossed her arms over her ample bosom.

The bus chugged down Lombard Street, toward the Golden Gate Bridge, past the area where the Palace of

Fine Arts should have been. Designed for the 1915 Pan-ama-Pacific Exhibition, the Palace of Fine Arts with its Greek-inspired architecture was a sight to behold. I felt an affinity with the weeping ladies that graced the circumference. I looked for the female statues that topped the Palace's Corinthian columns, but I couldn't see them through the camouflage netting that now covered them.

"They've requisitioned the Palace to use as the motorpool. Can you believe that? It's a disgrace. At least they had the good sense to put camouflage on the weeping ladies." Mrs. Tolliver leaned over my lap and looked out the window, craning to see the tops of the statues, giving me a whiff of her unwashed hair in the process. They were invisible under their camouflage. "That way the Japs can't see them when they fly over. We don't want our fine buildings demolished by enemy bombs, like them in London."

As the bus headed over the Golden Gate Bridge, I watched injured ships, twisted-metal casualties of the war waged at sea, being pulled into the San Francisco Bay by tugboats.

Mrs. Tolliver explained that the wrecked ships would be dry-docked, where they would be repaired or scrapped for the valuable steel, a much needed resource during this time of war.

"Times have changed, missy," the old woman said. She leaned back into her seat and crossed her arms in front of her. "Bennett Cove ain't what it was when you left. Neither is Bennett House, but you'll see that for yourself."

We rode along in silence. Soon Mrs. Tolliver fell asleep, her head lolled to one side, her mouth open. She didn't wake up when the bus rolled into Sausalito, the last stop before the road that led over the hill and down to Bennett Cove. If San Francisco's population had increased during my time away, Sausalito had burgeoned. Scores of houses had been demolished at Pine Point in order to accommodate the huge shipyard which had changed the city's landscape and—by the looks of the crowd at the bus stop—increased its population. When the bus pulled to a stop along the main street, I pressed my face against the window, but couldn't see anything except masses of men, some in uniform and some dressed for manual labor.

A handful of soldiers got off the bus. One man, a civilian, trailed behind them, getting on. He took off his hat, smiled, and nodded as he handed the driver his fare. His eyes were the most intense shade of green I had ever seen, their vivid color accentuating the dark circles beneath them. Although his suit and tie were of the same fine wool gabardine that my father favored, his face had the pallor of someone who had not seen natural light in quite a long time. I recognized that pale skin. I suffered from it as well. He caught me staring at him, as he passed by on the way to an empty seat. I turned around and peered between the seats as he stowed his bag in the rack above. When he sensed my eyes on him, he looked right at me. Our eyes met. He smiled, his green eyes crinkling at the corners. I smiled back before turning around in my seat.

Soon the bus pulled away, and my thoughts turned to other matters, like Gran and how she would react to my father's summoning me home. I shook off this worry. I had come home at my father's suggestion. He would welcome me to Bennett House. Gran could do as she pleased. I wasn't leaving until I discovered what happened on the night of my mother's birthday—and death.

When the bus turned onto the two-lane road that led up the mountain, the chatter stopped. The road to Bennett Cove was narrow and twisty, a rocky wall on one side and a precipitous drop to the ocean on the other. There were no guard rails. A group tension, a collective hush, fell over the passengers. The only sound on the bus was the gentle susurration of Mrs. Tolliver's snoring. When the bus pulled into Bennett Cove and came to a stop in front of the old post office, I heard a collective sigh of relief among all the bus riders, except Mrs. Tolliver, who snorted a couple of times as she woke up.

ᘓᐁᘓ

The day was bright and warm, with a refreshing undertone of the fall chill that would set in when the sun went down. I stepped off the bus and took a deep breath, filling my lungs with salty sea air. A queue of soldiers poured out of the post office and onto the sidewalk in front of it. Others came out carrying bundles of packages and letters. Green military vehicles crept along the clogged street in the first traffic jam I had ever seen in my home town. The milkman, who still used a horse-drawn cart to deliver his cargo, headed back to the dairy. His horse, a gentle shire whose hooves were the size of dinner plates, pranced along the streets with his neck arched and his ears pricked forward. There wasn't a parking space to be found. At the end of Main Street, between the post office and the beach, rows of tents had been pitched. The window in the post office had the same poster I had seen all over San Francisco affixed to the door. "Loose lips sink ships! Please don't discuss military activities!" Next to it was another plea to purchase war bonds.

My green-eyed stranger got off the bus ahead of me. He walked up to an imposing black sedan, an incongruity next to the military vehicles and personnel. As he drew close, the back window of the car rolled down. My stranger open the door and slipped into the backseat.

"Do you want to use my phone to call your family?" Mrs. Tolliver asked. "They'll want to come and fetch you."

"No, thank you," I said, staring at the car as it pulled away. "I want to walk."

"It's a long way, dearie," she said, squinting up at me.

"I'll take the shortcut along the beach," I said.

"Good. You could do with some fresh air," she said. She reached into the burlap sack and handed me a jar. "Eat this vegetable soup. It will put some color in your cheeks."

She picked up her shopping bags and lumbered away from me, toddling on ankles that were swollen over the tops of her brown lace-up shoes.

*၄/ာ၄/ာ*

I kicked off my shoes and stepped onto the sand, savoring the warmth of the sun on my cheeks, the soothing rhythm of the waves as they crashed to the shore, and the tangy sea air.

"Hello, Sarah."

I turned, surprised to find Mrs. Kensington standing next to me. We had struck up a friendship at The Laurels, where her daughter was also a patient.

"Hello," I said.

"I'm glad I found you," she said, smiling at me. "I heard you had left and was sorry that we didn't get to say goodbye."

I set my valise down on the ground and shielded my eyes against the glare from the sun. Today Mrs. Kensington had on a simple black dress and the gold locket she always wore. Inside it was a picture of her husband, who died in 1918 of influenza, and her daughter. I had never seen the pictures, but Mrs. Kensington had told me that the locket held the pictures of her beloved family. *'I like to keep them close to my heart.'* She had on stockings and fine leather shoes, inappropriate attire for a walk on the beach. But I was glad to see her. Our friendship had sustained me during my time of grief.

"How in the world did you know I would be here?"

"They told me you had gone home," she said. "I was glad to hear that you had gotten out of that horrid place."

"I still don't understand why you've come all the way here," I said.

"I can explain," she said. She became serious. "You must be very careful, Sarah Jane. Things at Bennett House are very strange right now. I know you didn't push Jessica down the stairs."

"What? How can you know that? I don't even know what happened that night. I don't remember anything. Don't you read the newspapers—" I stopped myself before I said too much. Oh, what a fool I had been. "You people have no scruples, do you? My god, you've been lying to me. You must think I am so very stupid."

"I'm not a reporter. I'm here to help you. That is the only reason I am here. Oh, I've made a mess of it, haven't I?" She wrung her hands. Were those tears in her eyes? "I want to fix things, make it all right."

"You tell me who you are and what you know about my mother or I'm walking away," I said.

She didn't speak. Instead, she reached out and

touched my cheek with fingers that were icy cold. "I'm sorry I upset you, Sarah," she said, as she turned and walked away from me.

"Wait," I called after her. "How do you know I didn't kill my mother?"

She slowly turned around to face me. "It's just a feeling I have right here." She touched her heart as she spoke. "Go home, Sarah. When I figure out how I can help you, I'll be in touch."

I watched her for a minute before I picked up my bag and set out once again toward Bennett House. She was a smart one, I'd give her that. For a brief second, I was ready to believe her, to let her help me, to confide in her. What a disaster that would have been. I could see the headlines now. She got right to my sensitive spot. But while her behavior was unscrupulous and loathsome, no one had ever uttered those words to me: '*I know you didn't push Jessica down the stairs.*' Not Gran. Not my father. How could they? They didn't know.

I turned for one more look at this strange woman who acted as though she believed in me. She was gone.

'*I know you didn't push Jessica down the stairs.*'

The words kept repeating in my head as I trudged through the sand toward home. How desperate I was to believe that woman, to think that I might have an ally, someone who believed in my innocence and could help me prove it. How foolish. My heart sank. If one newspaper was onto the fact that I had come home, others would follow. We would have reporters camped out near our home, much like we did after my mother's death. I had come home, but had brought trouble with me.

I craved a bath, a cup of good strong coffee, and my bed. By the time the pitched gables of Bennett House peaked out above the trees, my shoulder ached from carrying my bag and my feet smarted from the hot sand. I put my shoes back on and stepped into the grove of old redwoods that circled the house, separating it from the dunes that led to the beach, then out of their protective shade and onto the shabby lawn. Bennett House loomed, tall and strong and timeless.

Weeds poked through the bricks that made up the walkway to the front porch. One of the shutters on the front windows had come loose and hung sideways on its hinges. The roses that grew on either side of the walkway had been neglected in my absence. They were overgrown and covered with dead flowers and brown leaves. The nasturtiums had gone wild and taken over the other perennials that grew along the foundation, their orange and yellow flowers bright and lovely. Fat lazy bumblebees hovered around them. The clematis that grew on the lattice near the front door had reached the top of the wooden structure and was now intent on weaving itself into the old copper gutters, which had turned a mellowed patina of green decades ago.

A large raised-bed garden had been planted on the sunniest patch of lawn, its pristine rows a stark contrast to the rest of the unkempt landscaping. I recognized what was left of peas, beans, tomatoes, and squash, most of which had already been harvested.

As I stepped away from the cover of the trees, a flock of gulls circled above me, as if to announce my presence. They called out to each other, cawing in harmony, with the Pacific Ocean as their accompaniment. I headed up the path, took the two steps up the porch, and paused for a moment before knocking on the massive wooden door. Would I be welcome? Or should I turn around now and run, while I still could?

I reached out my hand to knock as the door burst open. A woman I did not know stood before me on the threshold. She fumbled with a bag designed to hold a camera and several lenses. When she saw me, her mouth opened and her eyebrows shot up in surprise. Her flawless make-up accentuated her beauty. The dress she wore, a charcoal gray sheath, flattered her slim waist and narrow hips. An emerald-green silk scarf held her hair away from her face. Her eyes now traveled up and down my body, taking in my old and much-mended linen skirt, my blouse, now wrinkled from my trip home, and my hair, which had grown during my time away, and had now escaped from the clip that held it away from my face. I didn't speak. I just stood there stupidly, not quite sure what to say.

"You must be Sarah," she said.

"I am," I said, faking a smile. "Who are you?"

"We wondered when you would show up." She ignored my question and stepped away from the door, holding it open for me. "They called to tell us you had left. I know Jack told you to come home, but you could have called us, let us know when you were going to arrive. How did you get here, by bus? Did you walk all the way from town?"

She didn't let me speak.

"You may as well come in." She stepped aside and allowed me to enter my own home.

As we stood for a moment in the foyer, I took in the parquet floor, the sweeping staircase that led to the second story, and the mahogany table that had graced the center of the room since the house was built. For as long as I could remember, a crystal vase the size of a small child had graced the center of the table, always filled with a huge bouquet of flowers. Today the table was bare and the crystal vase that had rested upon it was gone. I ran my hand over the smooth wood, surprised at the dust that had been allowed to accumulate on top of it.

"It's hideous, isn't it," the woman said.

"I'm rather fond of it," I said.

She smiled at me. "I wanted to get rid of it, but your father wouldn't hear of it. I tried to have it hauled up to the attic, but it wouldn't fit up the staircase."

Who was this woman?

A shotgun rested by the front door. She saw me eyeing the weapon, so out of place and strange.

"That's for us to shoot invaders," she said as she shut the door and locked it, sliding the dead-bolt home with a resounding click, something I had never done in my entire life. She headed down the long hallway toward my father's study, not bothering to see if I followed.

The inside of the house had changed. Furniture had been rearranged; pictures had been taken off the wall and re-hung. My father's office, a large room just off the library, was still full of the books that he and my mother loved. They were everywhere, jammed without order into the floor-to-ceiling bookcases, stacked in piles on the floor near the window, and on the credenza behind my father's desk. The silver inkwell that had belonged to my grandfather was gone, along with the pictures of my mother and me that had rested on his desk for as long as I could remember.

I stood in the doorway, watching my father as he sat at his desk, hunched over one of the many pads of paper that were piled next to the brass banker's lamp. His reading glasses had slid down his nose, and when they did fall off, he reached for them while continuing to read, oblivious to us interlopers in his literary domain.

When the woman who had opened the front door slipped behind my father, wrapped her arms around his neck, and kissed the top of his head before snuggling cheek to cheek with him, my stomach clenched. Still reading, my father reached out and grabbed her hand. Something was very wrong.

"Darling, someone is here to see you."

My father looked up. When he saw me, his eyes opened in astonishment before they relaxed into relief. "Sarah, thank God," he said. He took off his reading glasses, set them on his desk, and came toward me with open arms.

I stepped into them. My father hugged me. When he moved away from me, he put both hands on my shoulders and looked into my eyes. "I'm so glad to see you." He studied my face. The woman stood near his desk, her arms crossed over her chest. "I think it's time you came back to the fold," my father continued. "It's been a year. Can you believe that?"

"It's good to be home," I said.

"I see you've met Grace." He walked over to the woman and put his arm around her.

"Not officially," I said. "Hi."

"Grace and I—" My father hesitated.

"I'm Jack's wife," the woman said.

# CHAPTER 2

After blurting out the words that my father wouldn't say, Grace moved away from him and walked to the fireplace, which in my absence had been filled with ferns.

I almost laughed out loud at the absurdity of that. Ferns? In the fireplace? "Congratulations. When did this happen?"

He went back to his desk and sat down. "About eight months ago. I know it's a surprise. I had every intention of telling you, but a letter just seemed so impersonal."

"You could have visited me," I said.

"No." My father shook his head. "The doctor told us that it would be best to leave you alone for a while, to see if your memory would come back on its own. Sarah, I don't blame you for being angry. We didn't want a big ceremony or a party. We just—"

"We just wanted to be married, Sarah," Grace interjected. "We didn't have a big ceremony, just a few close friends. I hope you can understand and forgive us for not including you. You were away, and we thought it best that you stay at The Laurels so you could get better."

We were all silent for a moment, my father looking at the papers on his desk, out the window, anywhere but at me. When the phone on his desk rang, I jumped.

My father answered. He listened for a few seconds and then spoke. "She's here. She's fine." He paused before he said, "Thanks," and hung up the phone. "Come sit over here, Sarah." He beckoned to one of the chairs that sat before his desk.

He didn't ask Grace to sit. She continued to stand behind him, as though they were a united front, as though I were the intruder.

"Does Gran know you summoned me home?"

We had all suffered when my mother died. I had lost a mother, but Gran had lost her only child. She doted on my mother and, although she didn't always agree with my mother's free-spirited attitude, she still loved her daughter with a singular devotion that continued to surprise me. For my father's part, he had allowed his mother-in-law to live in the small gardener's cottage, and this arrangement seemed to suit everyone.

Gran had her own place to live near her daughter,

and my father didn't have his mother-in-law continually underfoot.

"She knows, but she wasn't happy about it. I'm just being honest, Sarah. I've missed you, and I'm anxious to put that night behind us. Have you been able to remember anything at all?" My father wanted me to remember that night, too.

Finding out what happened to my mother that horrible night would set us all free.

I shook my head. "No, but not from want of trying. I don't remember anything about that night, nothing at all. Maybe now that I'm home, I will start to remember."

"We may never know what happened, how Jessica came to tumble down the stairs. We may have to accept that she tripped."

"Which means the cloud of suspicion will hang over my head forever," I said.

"That's a little dramatic." My father leaned back in his chair, his movement forcing Grace to step away from him.

"I need to clear my name," I said. "Everyone in Bennett Cove thinks I am a murderer."

"I understand," my father said. "If there's anything I can do, if you want to talk, I'm here."

"Thanks," I said.

"Jack, don't you think she should be under the care of a doctor? What if she does something while we are asleep in our beds?"

My father ignored his young wife, as though she hadn't spoken at all. "You're welcome here, Sarah. I've missed you and I'm glad to see you," he said. "Now let me tell you what we've got planned for this evening."

I waited, not speaking, taking in everything that had happened during my absence. My father's successful foray into the world of mystery writing and his marriage proved that life had gone on without me.

I took a deep calming breath, a technique I had learned at The Laurels, pulled it deep into my belly, and exhaled slowly.

"Are you okay?" My father looked at me with the usual concern and worry, but there was something else, another emotion that I couldn't read.

"I'll be fine. I just need to get used to being here." I stood up. "Thanks for encouraging me to come home."

"I am going out to shoot some film. I'm headed up to the ridge if anyone wants me. Do you want me to go to the post office," Grace asked, "or will your assistant go for you?"

"Assistant?" I asked.

"After you left, I needed some help," my father explained. "He schedules my appearances, tends to hotel reservations and whatnot."

"He's kept busy answering your father's fan mail," Grace said. "He gets piles of it." She nodded to a burlap sack in the corner behind my father's desk that burgeoned with unopened envelopes.

"It's nice to have someone tend to those things," my father said. "It frees me up to focus on writing."

"Does he stay in town?" I asked.

"No," my father said. "As a matter of fact, he's been staying here. There are no accommodations in town. The inn has been booked solid due to the housing shortage in the city. It's easier for Zeke to live here."

"I think he's a spy," Grace said. "Did you hear that we have a ring of spies in Bennett Cove?"

"I hadn't heard," I said. "They didn't allow—"

"I'm sure Sarah's exhausted from her trip home," my father said.

"Of course she is. Apologies, Sarah. If you'll follow me, I'll show you to your room." She walked toward the door with her head held high.

*Show me to my room? Was my stepmother serious?*

"I'm glad you're home," my father said. "I'll see you at dinner." He turned back to the papers laid out on his desk.

I followed Grace into the foyer, picked up my suitcase, and headed up the stairs.

"I'll see myself to my room, if you don't mind."

I took the first three stairs.

"Sarah?"

"Yes?" I rested my hand on the banister, and faced her.

"I expect you to dress for dinner. We will have drinks at 6:30 in the drawing room," she said.

"Grace, this is my home, too," I said. "Just so we are clear."

I turned my back on her and headed up the stairs.

‹›‹›

The air in my room was musty and stale. I pulled open the thick black-out curtains and threw open the windows, letting the sea air come rushing in at me. The mattress on my bed had been stripped of sheets and co-vers. The rosewood dresser, armoire, and bedstead that had been in my room since the house was built had been pulled away from the wall, as if someone had tried to move the heavy furniture until they discovered the im-possibility of that undertaking. I went to my dresser, pull-ing open one drawer after another—all empty. I threw open my closet doors.

Aside from an old coat and an empty hat box, it was bare. Frantic now, I searched for my jewelry box, which had held a few treasured pieces that belonged to my mother. It was gone. The two pictures that I had hanging on the wall, seascapes done in pencil by a local artist that were quite valuable were also missing, their absence marked by a square of bright paint in the spot where they had hung for years.

"What is going on around here?" I asked out loud.

"She took everything," a familiar voice said behind me. "She took all the beautiful things for herself, even your blessed mother's jewelry. She acts as if it all belongs to her, and your father lets her."

"Anca," I said, pulling the dear woman, who was like a mother to me, into my arms and hugging her tight. She smelled of lavender and the lemon oil that she used to polish the ancient furniture that my great grandfather had brought to Bennett Cove from England.

I pushed away from her and sat on the bare mattress. Exhaustion washed over me. Anca made the sign of the cross over her chest as she took a handkerchief out of her apron pocket and wiped her eyes.

"It is good now that you are home," she said. She opened my suitcase and started putting the few clothes I had taken with me away in the empty drawers. "I took a few things of your mother's before *she* found them, some good dresses, skirts, sweaters, and a couple pairs of shoes. You're mother wore beautiful clothes, God rest her soul, and you are close enough in size, thanks to the heavens. I will not have you dressing in rags."

"Thank you," I said.

"I am worried this party tonight, this reenactment, will come to no good. It's wrong. It's morbid." She forced a smile. "Never mind. It is good you are home."

The sight of the basket that Anca used to carry her fresh linens, a simple reminder of the day-to-day chores of normal living, tugged at my heart strings.

We made my bed, tucked in the sheets with hospital corners, and covered everything with a chenille bedspread that was old and shabby and just fine with me. We didn't speak. We didn't have to.

"Your father is not so happy. He works all the time, more than he used to. He knows he has made a mistake marrying that woman," she said. "At night he paces his room. Back and forth, back and forth he walks."

"He surprised me, getting married like that," I said.

"Be careful of her. She uses her charm to manipulate." Anca stood with her back to me, staring out the window at the waves in the distance. "She wasn't married a day when she went through your closet and your drawers. She tried to take your dresses, the best ones from I. Magnin, but I grabbed them from her and told her I would tend to them.

"She makes me wear a uniform at meal times and won't let me eat at the table, like I have for twenty-five years. She is a witch. She has cast a spell on him. You smile at me like I am crazy," she said. "She's been spending money that your father doesn't have. She buys things for the house and things for herself. The banker has been coming to the house, trying to come to an understanding about the overdraft." She plucked a stack of fresh towels out of her basket.

"At least they seem to be in love," I called after Anca.

"She's in love with money, that one."

ഗ്രെ

I walked down to the beach behind Bennett House and headed north. If I walked about three miles, I would reach the steep, rocky cliff wall. On this October day not a single cloud floated in the sky. The sun beat down upon me, its warmth seeping through my skin and into my bones. I had changed into a simple yellow cotton dress, over which I wore a heavy wool sweater. It was cold, but the chill and fresh air felt wonderful. I wriggled my toes in the sand, while over my head the gulls continued to cry as they soared and dipped close to the water. Every now and then, one of the gulls would swoop down and fly away with a fish wriggling in its beak. At the water's edge, sandpipers landed in flocks, searching for food left by the retreating sea. When I got close to them, they flew away in unison, chastising me for the interruption. I walked along, savoring every step, every moment.

The lifeguard stations, which were positioned every hundred yards or so along the beach, were now manned by military personnel, who watched the sea with binoculars looking for the Japanese submarines that lurked under the surface, the same submarines that had been trying with some success to sink our merchant ships and had tried to open fire on our shores.

I looked up at the main lifeguard tower, a tall building with four glass walls, which provided a panoramic view of the ocean. I imagined the men in uniforms stationed there, tense and ready, should our shores be invaded.

I walked for about an hour, heading north on the beach toward the rocky cliff wall, where the road for cars and the sandy beach joined. The road ran parallel to the shore here. Soon I stumbled across an old farmhouse. It was a two-story, with a wrap-around porch and well-worn siding, which spoke of an old building that had been in place for decades. But this one hadn't. I had walked this part of the beach hundreds of times. This house was new. On closer inspection, I saw the windows, two by the front door, and two upstairs, had been bricked shut where the panes should be. Nestled behind the house was a barn, also constructed of the weathered siding, which had turned gray with age. But this barn had no doors or windows.

Behind these two buildings was another bigger structure with an iron door and small windows near the line of the room. The egress to the road was protected by a gate, which was now closed. A small sentry hut had been constructed near it. Two soldiers sat in the tiny structure, studying a clipboard. A black sedan came to a stop near the hut. The sentry stepped out, checked the driver's credentials, saluted, and opened the gate in order for the vehicle to pass through. Why not go up to the guard and ask what type of building this was? With a purpose to my step, I headed toward the hut.

"Put your hands up and turn around," a voice behind me said.

My heart started to pound. I did as I had been ordered and turned, holding up my hands. A young man, whose face was covered with spots, pointed a rifle at me.

"What are you doing here, ma'am?" he asked. The gun he trained upon me shook a bit.

"Just walking on the beach," I said. "I live over there." I nodded at Bennett House. "I didn't know that this was off limits."

"Private Marks, what in the world are you doing?" An older man came out of the compound by the entrance the truck had used. He walked over to us, kicking up sand behind him. "Stand down, Private."

"Sir, yes, sir," the private said. He held his rifle to his side and snapped to attention, holding his salute.

"At ease," the man said. "You may go."

"Yes, sir," the young man said. He took off at a brisk pace toward the perimeter of the fence.

"I'm sorry about that," the man said. "This area is off limits to civilians." He smiled at me as he extended his hand. "Colonel Matthews, at your service."

Colonel Matthews was a tall and lean man, with the burnished tan of someone who had spent a lifetime out of doors.

"I'm awfully sorry," I said. "I didn't know—I've been away—" I stammered like an idiot, not quite sure what to say.

"Best not walk here in the future."

A camouflage truck with a dozen or so soldiers riding in the back pulled up to the gate. The sentry let them in, and Colonel Matthews headed off without a backward glance.

"Yes, sir, of course," I said to his retreating figure.

I turned around and headed back toward Bennett House, not stopping until I reached the familiar stretch of beach closest to the house. The rhythmic waves of the ocean worked their magic on me. I sat down on the beach and stared at the waves, stretching my legs out in the sand. My legs had become pale during my time at the Laurels, where most of the day was spent inside under the watchful eye of the psychiatrist and nurses. I closed my eyes and must have dozed off, for when I awoke, my eyelids burned where the sun had beaten down upon them.

On a whim I stood up, shrugged off my sweater, and walked into the waves, not caring that my dress got wet. The biting Pacific Ocean cooled my sun-burnt calves. I kept walking into the shore break, letting the waves wash over my thighs, my hips, and my belly, exhilarated by the sensation of the cold salty water on my skin. I had taken a deep breath, planning to submerge myself, when strong arms wrapped around my waist and pushed me under water.

I tried to break away, but my assailant, who had pinned my arms to my side, had the position of strength. Although I kicked as hard as I could, desperate to get free of him, I couldn't escape and he didn't let go. We lost our balance just as a wave crashed over us. It knocked us off our feet and, after what seemed like an eternity, we rose from the foaming waves, sputtering and coughing, gasping for breath.

"What do you think you're doing?" I asked, doubled over, heaving for oxygen.

"Were you—I thought—I thought you were drowning." He bent over too.

"Drowning? I was swimming, or at least I was trying to swim." My legs were like rubber and gave out from underneath me after a few steps.

We staggered out of the water together and onto the sand. I collapsed. He sat down.

"I need to take more exercise," the man gasped.

We sat next to each other like that for a minute or two, both of us grunting and gasping and coughing, as we recovered from our ordeal. The man's hair, longer than what was fashionable, clung to his head in water darkened tendrils. When he looked at me, I recognized him right away.

"I saw you on the bus," I said.

He was doubled over, his face a grimace of pain.

"Are you okay?" I asked him.

"Cramp," he said. "I'll be okay in a minute." He closed his eyes and lay back on the sand.

I studied his face as he lay there. He had fine cheekbones and full lips. The stubble on his strong jaw was the same honey gold as his hair. He sat up, still trying to catch his breath. "What were you thinking, going into the water in your dress?"

"I hadn't planned on going in the water at all, but it felt so lovely, I just decided to—" How ridiculous I sounded. How in the world could I explain that all I wanted to do was swim?

"Decided to be spontaneous?" He finished my sentence for me.

"I suppose," I said.

After a few minutes, he stood and held out his hands. I took them without hesitation. He pulled me to my feet and continued to hold me, supporting me as I tested my legs, and once they were steady and I no longer needed him for support, I still held on, not wanting to break the connection between us. Heat radiated off his body. It pulsed through his hands and into me. He was warm and different, and I found myself mesmerized by those green eyes.

"I'm sorry if I scared you," he said, his voice soft and deep.

My body's involuntary response to him took me by surprise. "I need to go. Thanks for almost saving me." I let go of his hand. The heat of his touch lingered.

"Any time," he said.

I headed up to the dunes toward Bennett House. When I turned to look at him, he was sitting in the sand, gazing out at the sea.

# CHAPTER 3

Never mind having a gun pointed at me, I was still smiling from my encounter with the green-eyed stranger when I walked into Bennett House. Not wanting to explain my wet clothes, I avoided my father by going in the kitchen door and up the servant's staircase. Once in my room, I slipped out of my wet clothes and stood in my underwear, drying my hair with a towel, when my stepmother burst through my bedroom door without knocking. She held a lit cigarette in a long, black holder. She exhaled and a giant plume of smoke filled my room.

Anca had brought in a chair while I was at the beach, a shabby old thing, covered in an ancient and out-of-fashion Victorian chintz with giant roses growing on their vine. She had tucked it in the corner near the window and topped it with a mohair throw that my mother had crocheted many years ago. Ignoring my near-naked state, Grace walked over to the chair, threw the mohair blanket on the floor, and sat down. She leaned back, crossed her long legs, and stared at me.

"I saw you holding hands with that man on the beach," she said. "Do you have any idea who he is?"

"Excuse me," I said, not trying to hide the sarcasm. "I'm not dressed."

I scurried into the bathroom and grabbed my old blue bathrobe—thankful that Anca had put it back on the hook. I wrapped the towel around my hair, twisting it into place on my head. Through the crack in the door, I watched as Grace stood at my dresser, rifling through my handbag, which I had left closed. When I came into the room, she stepped away and acted as though she had been looking out my window.

I snapped my bag closed and tucked it under my arm. "I would appreciate it if you would stay out of my room. I know you've taken my paintings and my jewelry. Will you return my things, or do I need to speak to my father about it?"

Grace sighed. "Listen, Sarah, I'm afraid we didn't get off to a very good start. I am sorry if I made you feel uncomfortable or unwelcome." Now she moved over to my desk, but rather than stare at the papers that lay on it, she affixed her gaze on her reflection in the small mirror that hung on the wall. She checked herself and fooled with her hair, which didn't need any attention. It was perfect as it was. "I've never been a stepmother before and am not quite sure how to go about it. I know we're very close in age, and it must be awkward for you, but I do love your father. I want him to be happy."

She had a tube of lipstick in her cigarette case. She took it out and applied another layer, even though her lips were already coated with cherry red. She rubbed them together and made the type of strange face that women often do when they gaze at themselves in the mirror. Satisfied with her efforts, Grace turned her gaze to me. "Of course you can have your things back. I had planned on painting in here and maybe getting you some new furniture." She paused for a moment, as if debating what to say next.

Her eyes lit on the dress Anca had taken and kept for me in her closet. It now lay draped across my bed, ironed and ready for me to wear tonight. Next to it were my dove gray suede slippers, and a brand new pair of stockings, still in the packaging.

Grace ran her finger over the fabric. "Where did you get those?"

"Anca kept them for me, bless her," I said.

"I would like to be friends, Sarah, but if we can't do that, let's at least try to get along, for Jack's sake."

She stood there a moment with her hand on my door, poised, beautiful, and sophisticated.

The only thought that ran through my head was, *What has my father gotten himself into?*

After I had put on dry clothes, I faced the inevitable and stepped out in the hallway. My mother's bedroom wasn't locked, so I slipped inside before Anca or anyone else saw me. My parents had always kept separate rooms, and I thought this was common until I went to summer camp and realized that everyone else's parents actually shared a bedroom. Not my parents. My mother loved her own space. We used to curl up in bed on rainy days when I wasn't in school, reading books out loud to each other—I stopped those nostalgic thoughts. She was gone. There was nothing to be done about it. With her absence, the room had become lifeless and dingy.

I flung open the velvet curtains and sneezed at the dust that was loosened. In the harsh glare of sunlight, I could see the dust angels in the sun's rays. Anca, too busy caring for Bennett House to tend to a dead woman's bedroom, hadn't dusted or cleaned in here in a while. I wondered if my father had wanted to preserve this room, a reminder of the wife who used to live here, the vibrant woman whose spirit had touched everyone she met. I ran my hand over the cotton counterpane on the four-poster bed, the embroidered roses now dingy with a year's worth of dust.

My mother's nightgown still lay across the bed, as though she had just left it there. The silver comb and hairbrush that my father bought her for a wedding present still lay atop the rosewood dresser with the pink marble top. Memories of the past washed over me. I saw myself as a small girl here in this very room.

I saw my mother, with her dark hair in pin curls and cold cream on her face, saying, "Go on, honey, jump on the bed. Get it out of your system. It is forbidden and you will never be allowed to do it again." She stood watching me as I jumped up and down, screaming with glee. I closed my eyes and wished for a stirring of a memory from the night she fell to her death. Even a glimpse, a promise of a memory to come, would do.

Nothing.

I walked over to her bed and picked up the night-gown, the cold silk slipped through my fingers like water. Clutching the gown to my breast, I closed my eyes and willed myself to remember what happened. Once again, I remembered nothing.

ഐരുഐ

The drawing room was empty when I went down-stairs to dinner. Determined to take advantage of the trag-ic reenactment of the night my mother died, I came downstairs half an hour before anyone else, hoping that just being in the room where my mother and I had spent so much time together might kindle some flame of my memory.

The ancient grandfather clock, an unreliable old

thing, chimed six bells as I entered the drawing room. Given the way Bennett House was nestled among the trees, most of the other rooms were cloaked in a darkness so dense that the lamps did little to dispel it. Not this room. In here, the sun dipped in the western sky, casting its warm glow through the old leaded windows and onto the walnut-paneled walls, infusing the entire room with light. When my mother was alive, we kept very little furniture in here, opting instead for big overstuffed pillows on the floor. My mother studied ballet and dreamt of a future as a principal with a major company until an injury forced her to give up her dream. This room with its bright light and expansive floor had been our studio. The ballet barre that used to be on the far wall had been taken down, and the room that was once empty and vast and so full of light was now tastefully furnished. Jessica Bennett's ballet studio was no more.

Now the only reminder of my dead mother was the crystal vases of flowers that were scattered about. Two pale yellow silk sofas, along with a handful of comfortable chairs in various light and cheerful fabrics were arranged around the westward facing window. Grace had added big silk pillows in white and yellow, which made the couches even more inviting. The new pillows spruced up the ancient sofa and hid the upholstery underneath, which had worn thin in places. There were roses from Gran's garden in the cut crystal vase on the coffee table and more flowers in various vases on the mantelpiece.

The blackout curtains hanging on all the windows were pushed aside now so as not to obstruct the last bit of sunlight.

Someone—in all likelihood, Anca—had salvaged the old mahogany drinks trolley from the attic. It now stood in the corner with a bucket of ice, a soda siphon, glasses, and an assortment of crystal decanters filled with spirits arranged on top of it.

The picture of my mother and me that had always held place of pride on the mantelpiece had disappeared from the silver frame. In its place was a picture of Grace and my father, on the day of their wedding. Grace had on an elegant lace dress. My father wore his tuxedo, his reading glasses, and a somewhat bemused expression, as if he were in a fairy tale and expected to wake up any minute.

I was still staring at the wedding photo when Hamish Wentworth, our family lawyer, walked into the room.

"Sarah Jane," he said, his arms open.

I got up and hugged him.

"Well, let's have a look at you," he said.

He pushed me away and looked me over from head to toe. I smiled and did a little pirouette. Hamish reminded me of an elf. He was short, with snapping blue eyes, which had permanent smile lines etched at the corners. He had a ready smile, a quick wit, and seemed to know everyone of importance.

He wore the finest suits—today's was an elegant

gray flannel with tiny white pinstripes—and belonged to all the best clubs. But to me he was just an old family friend and someone who I had always enjoyed spending time with. For as long as I could remember, Hamish had spoken to me as if I were grown up, even when other adults were put off by the only child at the parties my parents used to have.

"I'm glad to see you back home. We've missed you," he said.

"Thank you, but I don't believe you. I'm sure my stepmother wasn't too happy at my return."

"Give her a chance, Sarah. This is all new to her."

"So you approve of the marriage?"

"I wish your father happiness, and I can't fault him for finding love again."

"He's full of surprises," I said. "I had no idea he was a writer."

Hamish smiled. "And a good one at that. I've surprised him with a visit to see his latest work in progress. I'm his agent too, you know. His publisher is clamoring for the next Jack Bennett novel, and Jack is three months behind schedule."

"Is it any good?" I asked with a smile.

"Haven't seen it yet," Hamish admitted. "But it's been fourteen months in the making, so I'm sure it will be as fabulous as Jack says."

"You know he wrote me with the news that the mysteries he had written in college were going to be published. I had no idea they would be such a success," I said.

"Jack was always the golden boy. Even in college, everything he put his hand to worked out in his favor. They used to call him Lucky Jack."

"Hamish, what's going on with the bank? Anca mentioned an overdraft. Should I be worried?"

"No. His book is doing well. I've loaned him the money for the overdraft. In fact, I just gave him the check today."

"What happened?"

"He made a bad investment. Don't worry about it, Sarah. This isn't the first time your dad has lost a substantial amount of money, and it won't be the last. He takes risks, and when he wins, he wins big. But sometimes those risks turn out to be warranted and he loses his investment. I've known him for years, and he's always made it back. There's nothing to worry about, really."

"You know we are having a dinner in honor of Jessica's birthday tonight?"

"I know," he said. "I'm sorry I am unable to stay. Are you okay with this? It's not going to be too difficult?"

A part of me wanted to scream that, of course, I was not okay with this, but my desperation to get to the truth trumped all my other emotions.

"I'll be fine," I lied.

We stood together before the window, looking out at

the ocean, both of us conscious of the void, the gaping wound that haunted us since Jessica's death.

When Hamish spoke, it was as if he were reading my thoughts. "Jessica was one of the most free-spirited people I have ever known," he said.

I smiled at him. "She was."

"I would watch the two of you together and often think that you were the level-headed one, the adult, and Jessica was the whirlwind that no one could contain." He wiped his eyes with the back of his hand, took a deep breath before he continued. "I remember when you were just a little thing, and Jessica told you to call her by her first name." Hamish shook his head. "She always said she would rather be your friend than your mother."

"The looks we used to get. The post mistress yelled at me for not addressing her properly. One day, when I rode my bike to collect the mail, she took me to task for being disrespectful."

"Jessica's child rearing methods were unusual," Hamish said. "But you turned out okay."

"I'll take that as a compliment and say thank you," I said.

"I need to go." He looked at his watch. "I have a business meeting in San Francisco. I just wanted to say a quick hello to you before I left."

"It's good to see you, Hamish," I said.

"Come have lunch with me when you are in the City. And Sarah, make sure your father knows that I need the draft of his manuscript in three weeks. He's horribly behind schedule."

"I'll try," I said.

We both heard the sound of Grace's high heels clicking on the floor, getting louder as she drew near.

"That's my cue to leave." He kissed my cheek, and when he was close enough, he whispered, "Don't let her push you around."

Grace, who had dressed in a midnight blue chiffon dress that flattered her figure and coloring, swept into the room, and air-kissed Hamish. If he didn't like Grace, he certainly didn't let on.

He air-kissed her in return, then stepped back to admire her ensemble. "You look gorgeous, as usual."

"Thank you, Hamish." She twirled around with her arms out to the side, showing off her dress. "It's an old favorite." She went to the drinks trolley and poured the proper measure of gin and vermouth in the shaker. "I'm sorry you can't stay for dinner." She shook the drink and poured the icy gin into a stemmed glass.

"I'm sorry too," Hamish said. "Rain check?"

"Of course, any time. You know that you are always welcome."

"In that case, I'll bid you both goodbye and see you again when Jack's book is finished."

Grace and I settled on the sofa. I spoke before the silence between us became awkward.

"So how did you come to settle in Bennett Cove?"

Small talk was in order. I didn't trust myself to do anything but ask innocuous questions.

"You mean how did I meet Jack?" Grace kicked off the dainty slippers that she wore on her tiny feet and tucked one leg underneath her. She sipped her gin and gazed out the window. "We met at the Sand Dollar. I was working as a waitress and your dad came in for dinner. We struck up a conversation and, soon, he was dining in the restaurant every night. One thing led to another..." She sighed. "And here I am."

"My father seems—"

"Excuse me, miss." Mrs. Tolliver stood in the doorway. She wore a floor-length purple dress that hung on her stout body like a sack. On her feet were what she called her good shoes, patent leather pumps that would have been fine if the toes weren't so scuffed and there wasn't sand along the place where the sole met the leather. She had an emerald green hat with about four too many feathers. Over her shoulder was the burlap bag that went everywhere with her. "I'm to serve at table tonight. I just wanted to let you know I'm here if you need anything. Hello, Sarah Jane."

"Hello," I said.

"How in the world did you get in?" Grace asked.

"Through the front door like I always do."

"And Anca asked you to come and help her?" Grace stood up and moved to the doorjamb where Mrs. Tolliver stood.

Mrs. Tolliver raised her chin in defiance. I prayed that she wouldn't say something she would regret. This situation had trouble written all over it.

"Grace, it's okay, really."

Grace turned on me with reddened cheeks, but she never spoke. She didn't get the chance. By some divine act of providence, my father saved the day by the simple act of walking into the room. I breathed a sigh of relief. He was dressed in a dinner suit I hadn't seen in a decade. The bow tie was crooked and his glasses rested on top of his head. He had cut himself shaving, and his cheeks had the familiar glow that came when he imbibed from the bottle of scotch he kept in his study.

"Mrs. Tolliver." My father bowed at the waist, took Mrs. Tolliver's hand, and kissed it.

"Oh, you." Mrs. Tolliver blushed and bowed her head. "I'm just off to help Anca then." Mrs. Tolliver headed to the kitchen, leaving little piles of sand in her wake, giggling like a school girl. Score one to Mrs. Tolliver. I only hoped that there wouldn't be retribution.

My father kissed Grace on the cheek, and it wasn't until Grace stood up from the couch that I realized my father hadn't come in the room alone. Behind him, dressed in an impeccable white dinner jacket, was my handsome stranger. His eyes opened with surprise as he recognized me, then he smiled.

"This is my assistant, Zeke," my father said. "Zeke, please meet my daughter, Sarah."

My stomach flipped and my cheeks went hot. I drained my champagne flute and went to pour myself a refill. "So we meet again," I said.

"Indeed," Zeke said.

My father moved away from us, as Grace pulled him into the corner and spoke to him—probably about Mrs. Tolliver's impudence at using the front door, which in Grace's mind was reserved for guests.

"I'm glad that we are going to get to know each other." Zeke took the champagne bottle from my shaking hands and poured for me. "After you left, I was wondering how I could figure out who you were, where you came from."

When he smiled his eyes crinkled in the corners. He smelled of an enticing combination of pine and musk. I lost myself for a minute, my eyes riveted on his dark blond hair as it curled around over the top of his collar. I was overcome with a strange physical longing, the likes of which I had never experienced before. It started in my stomach and burst out into every cell of my body. It seemed as though everyone in the room faded away, leaving Zeke and me in our own bubble. I wanted to kiss him, to feel those lips on mine. When I thought of the reaction that would provoke from Grace and my father, I laughed out loud, a crazy, reckless laugh, the sound of which caused Grace and my father both to stop speaking and stare at me, a puzzled look on both of their faces.

Mrs. Tolliver came in to announce dinner. She had

removed her hat and fixed her hair, and her manner was quite dignified.

Zeke smiled at me. "May I?"

I placed my hand on his arm and understood for the first time in my twenty-five years what the romance heroines meant when they were "walking on air."

The dinner was delicious and strange. Mrs. Tolliver served us with a grace and elegance that impressed. The wine was superb and, as we drank it, our tongues loosened. It was as though I was on a double date with my father and his new wife. We spoke of music and literature and books. No one mentioned the war, my mother's death, or my time at the asylum. By the time the meal was over, I was captivated by Zeke, by the possibility of what life could be like if one weren't bogged down by worries.

The four of us had gone back into the drawing room for coffee. Grace had put on a Count Basie phonograph record. Mrs. Tolliver had served us coffee, and we were dealing out the cards for a hand of gin rummy when someone pounded on the door.

"Who in the world—" I stood up to go answer the door.

"I'll get it," my father said.

"So do we play gin rummy for money?" Zeke asked.

Grace took a cigarette out of a sterling silver case. Zeke reached for the lighter on the table and was just about to light Grace's cigarette when Colonel Matthews, followed by three burly soldiers with angry scowls on their faces, stepped into the room.

"What's going on?" I asked.

"This is a private matter," Colonel Matthews snapped at me. His eyes locked on Zeke. "Are you Ezekiel Caen?"

"Yes, sir," Zeke's spoke in a calm and confident voice, but a sheen of perspiration broke out on his face. "I'll need you to come with me," the colonel said.

"What's this about? You can't just come in here and—" my father protested.

"This man is being taken into custody under suspicion of treason." Colonel Matthews nodded at the men, and they moved toward the table where Zeke, Grace, and I sat. Zeke stood up.

One of the men grabbed Zeke's arm. I couldn't see how he did it, but he moved like water and disengaged from the soldier's grip, leaving him surprised and then angry. When the soldier moved once again to grab Zeke, Zeke spoke. "I'll come voluntarily. Do not touch me."

"Shoot him if he tries to run." Colonel Matthews and his men followed Zeke out of the room.

After the front door shut, my father, Grace, and I stood there like a bunch of fools. None of us knew what to do next. My father broke our silence.

"I'm calling Hamish." My father didn't look at either of us as he spoke. He headed to his office, pushing his way past Mrs. Tolliver and Anca, who stood in the hallway, watching the entire scene with wide eyes and mouths agape.

"Anca, bring Sarah and I brandy." Grace came and put her arm around me. "Sarah, are you okay?"

Anca made the sign of the cross and headed back into the kitchen, Mrs. Tolliver at her heels. Grace and I moved into the library, which was now warm from the fire. I allowed myself to be led to the couch.

"You're in love with him."

"Don't be ridiculous," I said. "I just met him."

She rolled her eyes. "So you're naïve, too?"

The tears came unbidden.

Anca and Mrs. Tolliver brought tea and brandy and four cups. Grace didn't say a word as Anca poured out tea for all four of us, adding a generous dollop of brandy in lieu of cream and sugar. I don't know how long we sat like that. I slipped off into my own world, as I often did in stressful situations. Disgusted with my own inability to help and with nothing to lose, I stood up, startling Grace, who had dozed off in her corner of the couch.

"Where are you going?"

"To find out what's happening. If no one else will help Zeke, I will."

"What do you think you can possibly do for that young man that your father can't?"

I didn't know what I could do for Zeke, but I couldn't sit by and do nothing any longer.

e/oe/o

I barged into my father's study without knocking. The room was dark, save for the brass banker's lamp that rested on his desk, which cast a small circle of light on the old wood, but left the rest of the room in deep shadows. My father sat with his elbows on his desk, resting his head in his hands.

"Sarah? What's going on?"

"That's what I want to know. What's happened to Zeke? Did you reach Hamish? Can he help?"

"Zeke gave Hamish specific instructions. He contacted Zeke's friend in San Francisco, and this man assured Hamish that he would take care of everything. Don't worry. Your friend will be back here, safe at Bennett House before lunchtime tomorrow. And now, Sarah Jane, if you don't mind, I would like to go to bed." My father pushed his chair back and stood up. "It's been an exhausting day."

I stood on my tip toes and kissed his cheek. "Good night," I said.

"I'm glad you're here, Sarah. You belong here, home, with me and Grace."

e/oe/o

Once in my room, I kicked off my shoes, turned out the lights, and opened the blackout curtains, allowing the sea air and distant cadence of the crashing waves to lull me. I changed into my cotton pajamas, brushed my teeth, and got into bed, grateful at long last to be home in my own room, in my own bed. As soon as I lay down, the exhaustion hit. Soon I slept.

And dreamt.

I dreamt I was in an old house. Outside a big picture window was the stunning view of Alcatraz and the Golden Gate Bridge. In a dreamy fog, I surveyed the room, taking in the hardwood floors which were covered with plush carpets woven in rich jewel tones. Above me, the high ceiling was pristine white, with honey-colored oak beams. An old woman lay on a hospital bed, positioned in the middle of the room, her breath weak and raspy as though she were near death. Mrs. Kensington and I sat on chairs near her. In the slow motion and timeless way of dreams, I reached out and took the old woman's claw-like hand in my own.

"Aunt Joyce," Mrs. Kensington said. She had tears in her eyes as she gazed upon the old woman.

I closed my eyes and willed myself to wake up, but the dream wouldn't let me go. When I opened my eyes, I was still in the same room, but now Mrs. Kensington was gone, and I was alone with the old woman in the hospital bed. The room began to fill with mist. When the mist turned into acrid smoke, the woman lifted her head and spoke in a raspy voice. "I am dead. Save yourself."

Then the hospital bed, and the woman in it, disap-

peared. I was alone in the room. The smoke made it difficult to breathe. Just as I stood up, the chair I had been
sitting on burst into hot licking flames, which started to
spread around me. Through the thick smoke, I saw that
curtains now covered the big window. I hurried over to it
and, as I reached out my hands to push the curtains aside,
they too burst into flame.

The dry heat caught in my throat. My eyelashes
singed, and the smell of them burning made my stomach
roil. I recoiled and retreated back to the center of the
room. I circled, willing myself to wake up. On the opposite wall, two big wooden double-doors were as far away
from me as they could be.

I covered my face with my hands, took the deepest
breath I could, and ran toward the doors. My hand
grasped the brass handle. The heat of the metal seared my
flesh. I didn't care. I pulled with all my might, trying to
turn the burning metal handle. It didn't budge. The smell
of my scorched skin made me want to vomit, but my will
to live overrode everything else. The time for pain would
come later. The smoke had become dense now—too
dense for my lungs. I could no longer see the walls, the
curtains, or the door. I tried to hold my breath, until, desperate for life-giving oxygen, I gasped and gulped and
inhaled the noxious smoke. And died. Just as my spirit
left my body, I woke up.

એન્ટ

I sat up in bed, gasping and choking. I gulped, but couldn't take enough oxygen into my lungs. My nose ran and my eyes watered. My father and Grace burst through the door.

"Get her some water." He shut the window and drew the curtains before he flipped on the lamp and sat down in the chair next to my bed.

Grace did as my father instructed. By the time she came back into the room carrying the glass of water, my breathing had returned to normal.

When I reached out to take the glass from her, she gasped. My god, what's happened to her hand?"

Anca came in the room just then. She stood in the door jamb, behind my father and Grace. I opened my clenched fist and revealed what had caused the shock and horrific expression on my stepmother's face. On my palm, a vivid red welt in the shape of the door handle had singed my flesh. Seeing the wound brought home the pain of it. I winced.

"Call the ambulance," Graced barked at Anca.

"No," Anca said. She looked at my father. "Word of this will spread around town so quickly. She's just come home. I—"

"All right, enough," my father said. "Just leave it for now."

"You can't be serious," Grace said to my father. "You're going to protect her?"

For a minute it seemed as though my father's young

wife was going to faint. He let go of my hand and went over to her. She grabbed onto him.

"I don't know if I can handle this," she said, her voice rising in pitch and timbre, well on the way to hysteria.

My father put his arm around his wife's trembling shoulders. He ran his free hand through his hair, causing it to stand straight up. He had no slippers, just an old pair of mismatched socks that had been darned so many times they could no longer be worn under shoes. For a quick second I pitied him. Grace leaned into him, burying her face into his chest. He put both arms around her, but the look on his face was devoid of emotion.

"Do you need a doctor?" He asked me in a gentle voice.

I shook my head. "Let Anca fix it." My voice sounded scratchy and weak.

"How in the world did you burn your hand like that?" He still had his arms around his wife, who sobbed into his chest.

"You won't believe me," I said.

"Tell me anyway," my dad said.

"I had a dream," I said. I told him about the burning room, the curtains catching on fire, and my attempt to escape through the door, how the handle had burned my flesh. "There was a woman that I met at The Laurels in the room with me, Mrs. Kensington." I didn't tell my father that Mrs. Kensington had been on the beach yesterday, or that I now suspected her of being a newspaper reporter. "There was also an older woman, whom I've never seen before. She lay in a hospital bed. I think her name was Joyce—"

Grace cried out. She looked at me, her eyes wild with fear. Whatever blood she had left seemed to drain out of her face, leaving her pale as a ghost. My father supported her, as he turned her toward the door and out of my room, holding her close to him.

"I'm sorry," I called after them, "but I'm telling the truth."

"Come on," my father said to Grace. "Let's get you back in bed." They left the room together. Grace continued to sob as my father led her down the hall. He murmured sweet words to her, cajoling her as if she were a child, until the bedroom door shut behind them.

Soon Anca returned with the first aid kit she kept in the kitchen. She cleaned the burn on my palm, covered it with cream. Over that, she wrapped a gauze bandage. "We will watch for infection," she said. "I think it will be all right."

"I didn't do this."

"I know, dear. I know. Sarah, we need to talk about this. It's time that we addressed what you are able to do."

"I don't know what you mean," I said.

"You do know what I mean, Sarah. You dream, and you bring something from your dream with you when you wake up."

"I don't want to talk about it. Talking about it makes it worse. I've just gotten free of The Laurels. Please don't give them a reason to send me back there, Anca. I'm begging you, let it go."

"You cannot ignore this forever, Sarah Jane. You have a gift—"

"A gift? My god, don't tell me that this is a gift." I waved my bandaged hand in front of her face. "Everyone in this house thinks I'm crazy, that I should be locked up and kept away. I don't know what happened tonight. I dreamt of a fire. I woke up with a burn on my hand. I don't know what it means, and I don't care. I don't want to speak of it. Now, please, don't bring it up again." I turned out the light by the side of my bed.

Anca stayed seated on my bed. She didn't speak, didn't force the issue, her silence showing me I had hurt her with my harsh words. After a few minutes, she got up and went downstairs. I couldn't sleep. I tossed and turned, while my hand throbbed, reminding me of the precarious position I was in. I got out of bed, but rather than turning on the bedside lamp, I opened the black-out curtains and the window and looked out at the dazzling full moon.

Black-out be damned. If the Japanese submarines which cruised the shores of California, Washington, and Oregon wanted to fire their guns on us tonight, the light of the moon would show them the way. I stood near my window for a long time, staring out into the moonlit night. The sea air soothed away my pain and anguish, as it always did. I filled my lungs with it, but the burn on my palm still throbbed. I took the pain remedy that Anca had left for me, swallowing the pills with the glass of water that sat by the side of my bed.

I was ready to close the window and settle in for the night, when the front door opened beneath my bedroom. Using my good hand, I positioned the chair so I could stand on it and see down into the drive below me. There, in the moonlit night, someone—I couldn't tell who it was as they had on a black cap and a long dark coat—left Bennett House and hurried toward the main road that led to town. Who in the world was it? Where were they going? Part of me wanted to go after them, but I knew better than to head outside alone after taking pain pills. For once in my life, better judgment prevailed.

# Chapter 4

I fell asleep with my window open and woke up shivering from the cold air coming in from the sea. The flimsy chenille bedspread Anca had given me did little to dispel the chill. I would need the heavy blankets soon. The smell of apple turnovers baking in the Aga wafted up the stairs and made my stomach growl. I got out of bed and slipped into the dressing gown that hung on the back of my bathroom door. I belted the robe as best I could with one free hand, thinking of the steaming coffee and delicious pastry that awaited me in the kitchen.

On the floor lay a note from my father. He must have slipped it underneath on his way out this morning.

*Sarah,*

*I had news that Zeke will be coming home*

*this morning. I thought you would want to know. I*
*am off to San Francisco for a morning meeting.*
*Should be back after lunch. I left a copy of my*
*book on the desk, in case you want to read it. (I*
*hope you do.)*

*Feel better, daughter. Let's make a point to*
*spend some time together soon, maybe a good*
*hike and a picnic? I'm glad you're home.*
*J*

Anca wasn't in the kitchen baking this morning. I
was surprised to see Grace doing the honors. Today she
wore a red dress covered with tiny white flowers, with a
fitted waist and a flared skirt. She had donned a matching
gingham apron to protect her clothes from the flour and
sugar and apples that now lay in piles on the chopping
block in the center of the room. Her hair was pinned up in
a bun, but rather than making her look like a frumpy ma-
tron, the classic hairstyle accentuated the exquisite line of
her cheekbones. I looked down at my comfortable but
tattered ensemble and regretted not dressing before coming downstairs.

"What a surprise," I said, trying to smile.

"Good morning," she said, pouring me a cup of coffee.

She made a point to ignore my bandaged hand. She
avoided looking at it altogether and didn't bother to ask
how I was feeling.

"In case you're wondering, Zeke got home this morning, around 5:30. I only know because I couldn't sleep, so I got up early and heard the commotion when they dropped him off."

Zeke chose this moment to join us.

Grace stopped talking. She held the coffee pot in mid-air, her mouth dropping open in a surprised "O."

She and I spoke at the same time.

"What happened?" I asked.

"What did they do to you?" Grace asked at the same time. "Jack told me they roughed you up, but I had no idea how badly."

Zeke's left eye was swollen into a red slit, surrounded by the inchoate blue of the bruise that would come. A nasty cut ran across his cheek, which had been covered with iodine and stitched closed. His bottom lip was split down the middle. He had somehow managed to shower, shave, and dress in a button-up shirt, a tie, and well-pressed trousers.

"How about some orange juice?" I asked. "Can you drink fluids, do you think? We may have a straw somewhere. Or do you want coffee—" I talked too much, desperate to fill the silence before it became uncomfortable.

"Orange juice, please," Zeke said to me. "What happened to your hand?"

"It's a long story," I said, praying that he would have the grace not to push.

"You can tell me some other time," he said. "As for

this," he indicated his damaged face, "I'd rather not speak of it. Not today anyway."

"I understand," I said.

"Sarah was quite worried about you last night," Grace said. She opened the oven and looked in at her pies. "Would you like some breakfast? Anca is busy with the garden, so I can make eggs."

"No thanks." I didn't feel like eating. The bruises on Zeke's face, evidence of the brutality he had suffered, had taken away my appetite.

"I was actually talking to Zeke."

"Stay and have some breakfast," Zeke said. "Even if you don't want to eat, you can keep me company."

I had already stood up, embarrassed at my unkempt appearance.

"Sit with me."

How could I deny him? "I should probably go and dress first," I said.

"You're fine." He smiled while he spoke, that smile of his that put me at ease last night. It worked against me this morning.

Grace looked at Zeke as if to say, *You're kidding, right?* "So how do you like your eggs?" Her tone had become brusque.

"Scrambled, please," he said.

"Do you want some toast, too? I'll make you some," I said.

Grace didn't speak as she made the eggs. I bustled

around making toast, trying to stay out of her way. When the eggs were finished, Grace scooped them onto a plate. She carried them over to the table and set them down in front of Zeke. Without speaking, she took the pies out of the oven, set them on the rack to cool, and left the kitchen without a word. I set the toast in the rack and carried it, along with the butter and some blueberry jam to the table. Zeke buttered two slices and handed them to me.

"Thanks," I said.

He put his fork down and patted his mouth with his napkin, avoiding the cut on his lip. "Are you going to be okay?"

"I think so. Are you?" I smiled.

"I think so," he said. "Sarah, about last night—"

"You don't have to tell me. I understand some things are best left private."

"You need to know that I would never do anything to betray my country. You believe me, don't you?"

"I do."

"Well, if you want to talk, I'm a good listener." His eyes glanced at my bandage, before they met mine. "It'll be okay, Sarah."

"I don't know about that."

Zeke reached across the table, placed his hand on my forearm. The heat of him seared through my clothing.

"You have quite an appetite." I pulled away from him. When I broke our physical connection, my reason came back.

"I'm recovering from a breakdown. It took a long time for me to get my appetite back. Now I can't seem to get enough to eat. It's a long tale of woe, Sarah." He nodded at my bandaged hand. "Maybe in time, we can share our battle stories. I am sure yours is more interesting than mine." He smiled as he stood up and carried his plate and cup to the sink. "What are you going to do today?"

"I'm going to deal with my grandmother." I set my coffee cup in the sink next to his. "After that, I'm going to try to do some home repair."

"I sense complications with your grandmother," he said.

He added detergent to the water that ran into the sink, grabbed the dish cloth, and got busy with the washing and rinsing of our dishes. As he set them on the draining board, I made a feeble attempt at drying, another difficult task with one hand. Zeke took the towel from me and dried the dishes. I put them away as he dried. We worked together, moving around each other with ease, as if we had shared these domestic tasks for years.

"My grandmother and I have a tumultuous relationship. She seems to think that I am a child in need of constant supervision."

"I think she feels that way about all of us. She's an imperious lady." Zeke held up the coffee cups. I pointed to the cupboard where they belonged.

"They all think I murdered Jessica," I said, putting

into words what he already knew.

Zeke stood at the sink with his back toward me as he washed and dried the dishes. When I mentioned Jessica's murder, he set the dish cloth down and faced me. We stood very close, our eyes locked. My heartbeat quickened and my cheeks grew hot. Not the hot red that came from humiliation. No, this time, my cheeks were flushed with pleasure. My eyes focused on those wonderful lips of his, which were so near my own.

"I don't think you did anything to your mother, Sarah," he said.

He took my good hand in his. The heat of it made my heart pound.

"How do you know?" I asked.

"I know," he said with finality. "I can just feel it, here." He took my hand and placed it over his heart, which beat slow and steady in his chest. "Now I need to get to work." He let go of my hand, stepped away from me, and hung the dishtowel on its hook. "See you later."

And he was gone.

❧❧

Half an hour later, I stepped out into the crisp air. In the corner of the garden, Anca raked the fallen leaves into piles. Someone had retrieved my red Elgin Robin from the stable and leaned it against the porch. I put the bundle of goods for the Allied Families Charity in the carrying basket between the handle bars and headed to Gran's, paying careful attention to the potholes in the road.

Gran's cottage had no view of the ocean. Instead, her windows provided a view to her remarkable rose garden. I walked up the short flight of stairs to the porch, with its inviting wicker furniture and potted plants, and knocked on the door.

"Come in," she called out.

I entered—Gran hadn't taken to locking her own front door—and found her in her living room, standing at the antique secretary and speaking on the phone. Gran's living room was furnished with cast-offs from Bennett House. An old secretary that needed refinishing held Gran's books and her telephone. A chintz chair, similar to the one that Anca had brought to my room, sat before the fireplace.

On the floor next to it lay a pile of mending and a sewing basket. A copy of *The Arms of the Enemy* lay open on the coffee table. An antique horsehair sofa completed the furnishings. The floors were of bleached pine, the walls painted stark white. The floor-to-ceiling bay windows were designed to allow maximum light. The result was an open room, cheerful and timeless.

Since she had few modern conveniences, I always felt I had slipped into the late nineteenth century when I walked through Gran's front door.

Gran stood with her back to me and the phone cradled in her ear. She held up her hand, indicating that she would be finished in a minute. "I think you should do the right thing, never mind the money. I'm going to trust you to handle it," she said. The person on the other end spoke. "I'm giving you one week. If you don't handle it, I will. Very well, then, goodbye." She hung up the phone.

"Hello, Gran."

"Sarah Jane," she said. "You've come home."

"Yes," I said, "at my father's request. I was hoping you would have come to see me last night."

"I thought it would be best if I stayed away. I didn't want to give you the impression that I agreed with your father's decision to summon you." She stood rigid before me, scrutinizing me head to toe, with those hawk eyes that missed nothing.

"He summoned me because he thought I might remember something about the night my mother died if I were home."

"Well, have you?"

"No," I said. "I've been wracking my brain and can't remember anything. It's like a blank screen."

"Let's sit," Gran said. She beckoned me to the couch. "Do you want tea?"

"No," I said. "I want to talk to you about the night Jessica died. I need to know if you think I pushed her." I sat down on the sofa, sinking into the ancient cushions while Gran sat down in the chair.

"Of course you didn't push her. I know that. Shame on you for needing to ask me. But you were headed for a breakdown after she died. You were walking around here in a daze, and you know it. I've already lost Jessica. I don't want to lose you, too."

She picked up a garment from the sewing pile. I watched for a second, as she stitched up a hole in a cotton shirt of my father's, repairing it with expert stitching. I always wondered why Gran did all the sewing, rather than have it taken care of by the myriad of seamstresses in Bennett Cove who would welcome the extra money.

"Ouch," she cried. She sucked on her finger where a needle had punctured it.

"Why don't you use a thimble?" I asked.

She threw the sewing into the basket on the floor. "Don't be condescending. What's happened to your hand?"

"It's nothing," I said. "Just a burn."

"You're not just saying that, are you? You didn't—"

"Stop it," I said.

"I'm sorry, darling, but I am so very worried about you." Gran picked up a small swatch of fabric from the overflowing sewing basket, which she twisted and folded while she spoke. Gran had always been energetic. She tromped the walking trails with the vigor of a teenager, but she had aged during my absence. The skin on her face was loose. Deep lines now traveled from the side of her mouth down to her chin.

"What's wrong, Gran? Tell me why you don't want me here."

She stopped fidgeting and held the fabric still in her lap, her eyes fixed upon it. She threw it into sewing basket on top of the shirt she had mended. She mumbled something under her breath and shook her head. Was Gran talking to herself now?

"Have you read your father's book?"

"Not yet. He's left a copy for me. I haven't had time to read it. You heard about what happened last night? About Zeke—my father's assistant—getting arrested?"

"I don't know why your father hired that young man. He seems useless. He's clearly had a troubled past. He skulks around as if he's afraid of his own shadow, but he's a sly one, you mark my words. He doesn't miss a trick. He turns up in the strangest place. I've often wonder if he—oh, never mind. I don't want to speak of him." She leaned back on the couch and crossed her legs. "We need to rationally discuss your future, darling. You don't belong here, Sarah, and you know it. Your mental health is questionable at best. You're not stable, and I find myself wondering what you're not telling me about your hand. Why can't you just trust me, move to the city, find yourself a nice husband, buy clothes, go dancing, and live your life? You've no business here. There's nothing for you in Bennett Cove, nothing but horrible memories. You've no friends here, and I don't know why you aren't bored to tears."

"You may recall I agreed to go away from here after Jessica's death because we were being hounded by news-

paper reporters, and I thought that you were sending me
to a spa, not an asylum." I would never forget or forgive
the way those same reporters had used their headlines to
sensationalize my involvement in my mother's death and
cast suspicion upon me. Although no charges were officially brought, the cloak of suspicion hung heavy on my
shoulders. It was difficult to defend my innocence, since I
couldn't remember a thing from the night my mother
died. But there were no reporters now, and I'd been invit-
ed home by my father. I intended to stay at Bennett
House until I remembered what happened the night Jessica died.

"Sarah, won't you believe me when I tell you that it
is not safe for you here? Not now?"

"What am I in danger of? Tell me that and I'll listen.
If the threat against me is real, I should at least know
what it is. Surely you can understand that."

"I didn't realize you could be so stubborn." Gran
walked over to her desk where a white envelope lay, addressed to her in a bold vivid hand. I couldn't see the return address. She held the envelope in her hand, stared at
it for a moment, then shook her head and tucked it away
in the top drawer of her desk, which she locked with a
key that she wore around her neck on a silver chain. "I
can't tell you, not yet. You're going to have to trust me,"
she said.

"No," I said. "You're going to trust me. If you have a
good reason for me to leave, tell me. Otherwise, I'm stay-

ing right here until I remember what happened that night. Then I will make a decision about my future. It's time I leave here anyway. Perhaps I'll go to night school and learn type writing. I could join the WAVES."

"The WAVES will not hire someone who has spent time in an asylum. Why won't you just go back to The Laurels, at least for a little while? Or we could get you an apartment in the city. Wouldn't you like to be around people your own age? You could start school now. Once you're in the city, you'll find a suitable husband. I'll see you have entry into the right clubs and parties. There is no need for you to work."

"I am not leaving until I remember that night. I need to be here, at Bennett House, to remember," I said, catching myself before I told her I didn't want to leave Zeke. How foolish that would have sounded, wanting to stay here in Bennett Cove because of a man I had known for twenty-four hours.

"It's that assistant of your father's, isn't it? You've conjured up some silly crush."

"Don't be ridiculous," I said. "I'm home to find out what happened to my mother. That's all."

"Then you and I have nothing more to say to each other," Gran said. "I pray that you come to no harm." She picked up her sewing again, dismissing me without speaking.

⚮

I burst out of Gran's house and jumped on my bike. Rather than ride on the main road to town with the automobiles, I opted for the dirt path, a shortcut which wound through the trees parallel to the beach. The wide trail was covered in smooth red clay, topped off with duff from the pine trees that provided the shady canopy above. In record time I reached the end of the trail and emerged onto Main Street.

Military vehicles, soldiers, and tourists crowded the streets. I rode through town, once again surprised by the throngs of people in Bennett Cove. A long queue of uniformed soldiers clogged the sidewalk in front of the bakery. They stood in line, waiting to buy the scones, cakes, and pies displayed in the glass cases. I stood for a moment near the sidewalk, holding my bike, when a group of school-aged children came wandering down the crowded walkway.

Two young girls in pigtails and fancy coats led the way. They had on their good white gloves and carried little purses. Three boys trailed after them, one carrying a baseball bat, the next one carrying two baseball mitts. The third boy carried the baseball, which he tossed up in the air and caught with his bare hands.

I smiled as they passed by. The girls smiled in return, but the boys ignored me, all but the third child. When he passed me, he paused, stopped tossing the ball in the air and said, "Spooky Sarah," in that taunting voice that children use.

"What are you saying?" One of the girls turned around and came back to the boy. "It's not polite to speak to adults unless you are spoken to first."

"Everyone knows she's a witch," the boy said. "Everyone knows she murdered her mother, pushed her down the stairs, and broke her neck. Everyone knows it."

"I'm sorry for my brother," she said to me. "He has no manners."

I smiled at her.

"Come on, Harry." The girl grabbed Harry's arm and started to pull him along. "If you can't behave, you can go home."

"She's a witch," Harry wailed. He allowed his sister to drag him away as he looked back at me.

"Oh, for heaven's sakes, Harry, everyone knows there are no such things as witches." She gave me an admonishing glance as she dragged Harry away.

His two friends had stopped walking. They stared at me, mouths agape. When they realized their friends had moved on, they took off running after them.

"Are you all right, miss?" A soldier young enough to still wear short pants stood before me. "You look a bit pale." When I didn't answer him, he spoke again, his voice full of concern. "Don't mind what kids say. They can be mean sometimes."

"I'm fine." Bitter tears threatened to spill down my cheeks. I wanted to run after those children, buy them sweets and show them that I wasn't a witch, assure them that the rumors were false. I was a pariah in Bennett Cove. The small town gossip would never change. If I wanted to get away from it, I would have to leave.

"I'll be off then," the young man said.

I was about to get on my bike and ride the rest of the way down Main Street to the school house, when I saw Zeke walking down the street, carrying a brown attaché case. He moved like a cat with an equal measure of tension and grace. I ducked into the doorway of the five-and-dime and watched as he went into the lobby of the Bennett Arms.

Curious, I situated my bike in one of the new racks near the post office. Careful not to be seen through the lobby window, I crossed the street, thinking I could slip inside and get a look at whoever Zeke was meeting. If he happened to see me, I would tell him I was running an errand for Anca. Pleased with my plan, I walked toward the hotel.

The same black sedan I had seen yesterday at the bus stop rolled up to the curb, then it turned into the service alley on the side of the hotel. I slipped through the door into the vestibule where the hotel guests registered.

On the far side of the vestibule area, an arched doorway led to a common area where the guests could read the newspaper or sit before the fire. I tucked myself into the window seat by the clerk's desk.

From this vantage point I could see into the common area, a high ceilinged room with a huge fireplace and an array of comfortable club chairs arranged in "conversation areas" around low tables.

A sweeping staircase ran up one wall. Zeke had chosen the chairs tucked away near the staircase, the most private place in the room. I pretended to be engrossed in the newspaper, but all the while my eyes sought Zeke. When the man from the black sedan opened the lobby door and came into the room, I held up the newspaper to cover my face.

After he passed, I peered over it and got a good look at him, memorizing as many details as I could. I took in his thick black hair and the fine suit. Power. It crackled off him like heat lightning. Zeke rose from his chair and greeted the man like an old friend.

"May I help you, miss?" The clerk came out from the private area behind the desk, startling me. He squinted at me through his thick spectacles. "Oh, hello, Miss Bennett. I didn't recognize you."

"I was just leaving. Thanks just the same." I hurried out of the hotel and took off on my bike, grateful that Zeke hadn't seen me.

*** 

The Bennett Cove schoolhouse had been built in 1890 and hadn't changed much in the fifty years it had been standing. Its white walls needed paint, but the building proper had withstood flood, wind, and storm. A wrap-around porch encircled the entire building. A flower garden, which the school children planted and tended, was now filled with fall vegetables and mums in assorted colors.

Since I had been schooled at home by a live-in governess, the schoolhouse didn't hold the fond memories for me that it would for the local children. I hadn't been educated with the general population. That wouldn't do, not for someone of my station—Gran's words and ethos, not mine.

I leaned my bicycle against the mailbox in front of the building and headed up the muddy path to the schoolhouse, the parcel for the Allied Family Charity under my arm. On the porch, two signs made of heavy blue paper pointed in two different directions, one way to the Allied Families Charity collection point and another way toward the ration book office.

Anxious to get rid of the bundle of clothing, I headed toward the office that handled Allied Family's donations, when a voice startled me.

Mrs. Kensington appeared out of nowhere. "Have you read your father's book yet?"

"Hello to you, too," I said. "Do you always just appear out of nowhere?"

"I'm sorry. I'm not used to this and everything is a little fuzzy for me."

"Do you want to get a cup of coffee? We could go to the Bennett Arms and sit in the lobby," I said. Two could play this game. If she were a reporter, I would find out.

"Your young man is there," she said, smiling. "But no, I have to be somewhere." She put her hand on my arm. "Read your father's book, Sarah. It will help you remember."

"Remember that night?" I asked, incredulous.

"It's not going to be easy," she said, "but your memory will come back. And when it does, you must be very careful."

"I had a dream of a fire. You were in it. I woke up with burns on my hands," I held up the bandage for her to see.

"I'm sorry about that," she said. "There's so much to tell you, but I'm not sure where to start."

"How about telling me why you're here and what you know about the night my mother died."

"I can't tell you now." She looked over her shoulder. "I have to go. Be strong, Sarah. All this will come out right in the end." She turned and walked away from me, as she had done before.

Time stopped. I couldn't move or speak. My feet were riveted in place as I just watched her walk away, unable to call after her, unable to grab her arm and force her to tell me what she knew, and how she knew it. She had spoken with a conviction that I found frightening.

I shook my head, as if the movement could bring some sense of order to my day, but was still a little un-hinged when a familiar looking woman in a blue dress, also dressed for the city in white gloves and a hat, walked up to me. "Miss Bennett, you look a little lost. Can I help you find something?"

I had met this woman at one of my mother's charity luncheons, but I could not recall her name. "No, thank you," I said.

"You probably don't remember me. I'm Mrs. Jones, Mrs. Edgar Jones. My husband and I donated the Limoges pieces to the charity auction your mother had."

"Of course, Mrs. Jones, it's nice to see you again."

"May I ask you a favor? I hope you don't think me forward, but do you think your father would speak at my book club? A few of us ladies get together to discuss art and literature. The ladies would welcome an appearance by Jack Bennett. Why, you could come, too."

"He has an assistant that keeps his calendar. Perhaps you could call?"

"Okay. I'll do that," she said.

"It was nice seeing you again." I forced a fake smile and indicated the parcel in my hands. "I'll be off now."

A small hut with a Dutch door had been constructed behind the school. Beside the hut, a large cargo container sat with its door open, the rows of stacked packages ready and waiting to be shipped overseas. Inside the hut, Mrs. Tolliver sat, reading a *Life Magazine* that lay open on the counter before her, and knitting something pink and fluffy, with such expertise that she didn't need to look at her stitches.

"Hello, Mrs. Tolliver."

"I see you've got roses on your cheeks, girl. Coming home was a good decision, yes?"

"Yes," I said, putting the parcel of knitted socks, wrapped in brown paper and tied with string, on the counter for her.

"So have you been in the sun or are you in love?" Mrs. Tolliver counted her stitches as she spoke.

"It's the beach, Mrs. Tolliver," I said.

"How do you like your new stepmother? She's a dolly, that one." Mrs. Tolliver set her knitting down and took the parcel from me.

"Please come for a cup of tea sometime. I'm sure Anca would love to see you." I waved and headed down the path toward the front of the schoolhouse, anxious to get away from Mrs. Tolliver's uncanny ability to see inside my heart.

"You keep your chin up," Mrs. Tolliver called after me.

# CHAPTER 5

My bedroom smelled of the orange oil that Anca used for polishing wood. A few of my mother's dresses, now mended and pressed, hung in my closet. Although my mother and I were both slender, I was much taller. Her dark, sleek hair fell in raven tresses down her back, and while my strawberry blond hair curled on good days, most of the time it frizzed uncontrollably. I couldn't count how many times I had heard, "You two don't look anything alike."

At the foot of my bed, one box remained unpacked. I opened the lid, expecting to see more clothes smelling of mothballs. Instead, I was surprised to see my sketch books and charcoal pencils. Seascapes were my passion, even though I had never shown any remarkable talent.

I was a dilettante who sketched for the pure fun of it.

I had just gotten situated on the top of my bed, with my sketch pad propped up on my knees, charcoal pencil in hand, when a flash of lightning tore through the sky, followed by a boom of thunder so violent that my bedroom windows shook.

The sky opened up and the rain fell in a solid sheet of water. Outside my window, the black thunderclouds hung so low over the ocean, they seemed to touch the water. I tried the lamp by the side of my bed. Nothing. Not surprising, as the electricity often went out during bad weather. I lit the lone candle in the silver holder that sat next to my bed. With my sketch pad propped up on my knees, I got busy with the box of charcoals. Once the sooty black cylinder rested in my hand, everything fell by the wayside.

&#x204A;&#x3E;&#x3C;&#x204A;

I dozed. When I woke up, I discovered the sketch pad had fallen to the floor. The charcoal I had used for sketching had also rolled off my bed, leaving a trail of black behind it. The candle had died out long ago, its wick burnt away to nothing. I pushed myself up, rubbing the circulation back into my arm, which was numb from having slept on it. My stomach growled. It had been hours since I'd eaten. Outside my window, the rain had stopped, and the sun reflected off the puddles in the driveway, like so many diamonds. I swung my feet to the floor, but when I saw my sketch pad lying open at my feet, I stopped short. Heart pounding, I bent over and picked it up, holding my breath as I laid it out on the bed before me. I had drawn a perfect portrait of Mrs. Kensington, my mysterious friend. My charcoal had captured her personality in the sketch, had committed the emotion, the look of pain and longing in her eyes to paper. It was the best sketch I had ever done and reflected a skill level that I would never possess. Worse than that, I had no recollection of sketching this woman.

I tore the portrait out of the sketch pad, folded it in half, and placed it in the copy of my father's book that lay on the table next to my bed. I tucked the book under my arm, thinking that I would toss the portrait in the first lit fireplace I came across, after which I would start my father's book and read while I ate lunch. Downstairs, the house was quiet. My father hadn't returned from his meeting and there was no sign of my stepmother or Anca. I made myself a sandwich, poured a glass of milk, and went into the library. The doors to my father's office stood open. Zeke sat at his desk and, by the light of an oil lamp, he made notes in the leather calendar that lay open before him. He had a typewriter set up on the desk and, before too long, started typing away, pecking at the machine with his index fingers. I sat in front of the fire and ate, trying not to disturb Zeke while he worked, glad to have him near.

I was about to carry my dirty dishes back in the kitchen when the phone rang, breaking the silence that had settled over the house. Zeke answered. He spoke in such a soft murmur it took me a minute to realize that he wasn't speaking English. At first his voice sounded agitated. He said something, paused, and listened. When he next spoke, his voice was more subdued, but I could hear enough to recognize that he spoke in German with the fluency of a native. Without thinking, I stepped into the room, curious about what I heard, curious about Zeke.

He sat on the corner of my father's desk with his back to the door. He turned toward me, his eyes wide at the shock of seeing me there, of knowing that I overheard his conversation. He recovered his poise quickly, then said in English, "Thanks for calling. I'll get back to you." He then hung up the phone. "Well, hello."

I couldn't speak. I stood there like a fool, clenching my book to my chest.

"Sarah, I don't know what you heard," Zeke said. He stood up and came toward me. The look on my face must have deterred him, for he changed course, walked back to his desk, and perched on the corner of it. "I saw you in the hotel lobby today." He smiled as he spoke. "Next time, at least come over and speak to me."

I attempted to back out of the room, as if I could turn back the clock and erase all that I just heard. Instead, I tripped on an ottoman that had been moved away from its usual spot against the wall. My father's book, which I had clutched to my chest, went flying. When it hit the floor, the portrait I had drawn came loose. It floated down, coming to rest face-up at my feet.

Zeke swooped down in one graceful movement and picked it up. "Did you draw this?"

"Yes."

"This is amazing." He studied the picture. "Who is she?"

"Her name is Mrs. Kensington."

"How do you know her? Is she a friend?"

"Not really. I met her at the—" I stopped myself before I told Zeke why I had been away and where I had been. "—at the place where I stayed while I was away."

He gave me back the picture. "You have real talent." He picked up the car keys from the brass dish on my father's desk, along with a pile of outgoing letters. "I need to take these to the post office."

After the front door closed, I remained standing in the doorway between my father's office and the library. The room was cloaked in an unnatural hush, the only sound the tick-tock-tick-tock of the old grandfather clock.

I walked over to my father's desk and sat down in his chair. The top drawer wasn't pushed in all the way. I pulled it out, reached into the back of the drawer, and took the brass key out of its hiding place. We referred to the big drawer on the left side of my father's desk as the family vault. It contained our family financial information, check books, banking ledgers, birth certificates, passports, property deeds, and anything else of value.

The smell of the musty documents assaulted my senses. I sneezed, but continued to pull the fusty papers out of the drawer. At the bottom, underneath the pile, lay a knife with a wooden handle, painted in bright purple, red, orange, yellow and green. The thin blade looked rapier sharp. I took it out of the drawer and laid it on the desk, next to the pile of paperwork that I had pulled out. I rifled through the documents until I found the statements from my own account, which contained the inheritance from my mother. I had planned on going to college, perhaps becoming a teacher, but my mother's sudden and traumatic death, and my reaction to it, put the kibosh on all my plans.

I took the piles of papers out and laid them on the desk. Clipped together were a batch of bills, the bulk of them marked "Past Due." I thumbed through the letters. Many were from the bank and had never been opened. A letter from New York Life caught my eye. I opened it and scanned it.

My father had taken out life insurance on Grace, me, and Gran. He had also bought a policy on his own life, naming Gran, Grace, and me as the beneficiaries. I noticed that policies had been purchased after my father's marriage.

The rain had started again and came down in a torrent. It beat upon the window panes. For a brief moment, the past came rushing back to me. Every sense in my body, including that niggling intuitive sense that had always gotten me in hot water, invoked the time when my mother was alive. The tears sprang involuntarily. The sob wracked my body and the grief that should have come after my mother's death bubbled to the surface now.

I lay my head down on the desk, cradled it in my arm, and let the tears flow. I didn't stop until a gentle hand squeezed my shoulder, and my father said in the soft voice he had always used to comfort me, "Sarah Jane, don't cry."

His kindness made things worse. My sobbing continued. All the while he stood behind me, patting my back.

When my tears were spent, I lifted my head and took the handkerchief that he offered me.

"Thank you." I wiped my eyes and blew my nose.

"Did you remember something about the night of your mother's—"

"No. It's still a foggy blur. I've been in her room. I've sat down in the spot where you found me that night, trying to remember something. The harder I try to bring back what happened, the farther away the memory seems."

"I'm here if you want to talk, if you remember something," he said.

"I just want to remember," I said. "It seems as though I know something important, but it's just out of reach."

"Where did you find that?" He indicated the knife that lay on the desk. "I haven't seen that thing in years."

I picked up the knife and held it out to my father, but he didn't take it from me. "I found it in the bottom of the drawer."

"It must be ancient. Would you put it back for me?"

"Sure," I put it, along with the papers I had taken out, back where I had found them. "Is it true that the bankers are concerned about your overdraft?"

"I suppose Anca told you," he said.

"She's very worried about it," I said, "and I saw the notices in the drawer. What's going on?"

"I made some bad investments," he said. "But there's no need to worry. My book is doing well. I'll have it all sorted out in a week or two. Hamish loaned me enough to keep the bankers happy."

"Is there anything I can do?"

"No, and there's no need for you to worry, really."

"Am I interrupting something?" Grace came in the room and kissed my father's cheek.

"No," my father and I both spoke at the same time. We smiled at each other.

"When will the electricity be fixed? This house is so dark and gloomy." Grace shivered and rubbed her arms as she spoke.

"It might be a while. The only electrician in Bennett Cove is off fighting the war. I've found someone to come from San Rafael, but he won't make it out here for at least a week. We'll have to make do with candles and oil lamps."

"Well, I'm going up for a bath. I'll see you both later," Grace said.

After she left, my father looked at me. "Join me for a drink before you go up to dress?"

"Sure," I said, surprised at the invitation.

My father walked over to the cabinet that had been situated in the corner of his office for as long as I could remember. He lifted the heavy crystal decanter and poured us each a finger of single malt Scotch. He had never included me in this ritual. I wondered why he chose to do so now.

He sat down behind his desk. I took one of the empty chairs across from him, sipping the amber liquid. It burned my mouth for a second, the sensation turning to numbness as I swallowed. Soon the white heat filled my belly, and spread through the rest of my body. I liked the feeling. I sipped again.

"This is pretty good."

My father smiled. "Ladies are supposed to drink sherry."

"Well, we both know I'm not much of a lady."

My father swirled his drink. "How's your hand coming along?" He nodded at my bandage.

"Much better," I said. "I hope to be in a simple bandage by tomorrow. I wish I could explain why this happened. I swear to you that I didn't do this to myself."

My father refilled his glass, holding the decanter to me. I shook my head and placed the empty glass on the desk.

"You believe me, don't you?" I needed to know where I stood with him.

"I think that you believe you didn't harm yourself." He sipped his Scotch. "Some things are not meant to be understood, Sarah. You know we are all concerned about you." His eyes rested on my bandaged hand. "You'll tell me if you remember something, won't you? I would like to know how my wife died."

"You'll be the first person I come to," I promised.

We both sat silent for a moment, all the unanswered questions hanging between us, until the ring of the telephone brought us out of our reverie.

My father picked up the telephone receiver and listened.

"Tonight? Atherton? I think I can make that. Excuse me one second." He covered the mouthpiece of the phone and whispered to me, "It's the Mills Club in Atherton, last minute speaking engagement tonight."

I stood up and made my way out of the room. My father's cheery voice echoing behind me.

# CHAPTER 6

By the time I made it up to my room, the hard driving rain had turned into a gentle shower which I hoped would lull me to sleep. It didn't. I lay on my bed, craving a nap and expecting sleep to come without effort. Instead, the burn on my hand throbbed. I tossed and turned and couldn't get comfortable. I gave up and trudged back downstairs for the book I had left in the office, and the daily paper, which I found on Zeke's desk, folded open to *Text of the Day's Communiqué on the Fighting in Various War Zones*—an unemotional tally of the victories and losses.

Zeke and Anca clung to every bit of news about the fighting that raged in Europe, keeping score as if that would change things. They could often be found in the kitchen, huddled together before the radio, listening to the grim news.

The news of the fighting depressed me—the bombings, the displaced people, not to mention the poor Jewish people who were suffering at the hands of Hitler. The grim reports trickled in through the press and caused Anca to worry about family members she was unable to contact. My father tried to pacify her. He took the time to talk her through her anguish and assure her that he would do anything he could to help her, and that communication during war is always difficult. Although she wanted to believe him, she was frightened and worried. The German Army was ruthless in the occupied countries. We read in the papers every day how innocent people were taken into custody by Hitler's Gestapo for no reason and never heard from again.

The good news—if one could call it that—were the 1,000 rescued Jewish children who were coming to America from France. I wondered why all the displaced couldn't come to the United States. Why weren't all refugees brought here for safety until Hitler was captured and dealt with? It wasn't like the United States wasn't big enough. We were a country of vast open spaces. We had plenty of room and plenty of resources. I didn't understand it. I never would.

When it came time to dress for dinner, I said a silent prayer of gratitude that our water heater was gas powered, so hot water was available, even if only for a few hours. In an effort to conserve fuel, we lit the pilot light in the afternoon, so everyone could bathe. I languished in the tub until the water turned cold and the skin on my fingers and toes wrinkled.

I emerged, wrapped in my thick dressing gown, with a towel around my head. In my room, a fire burned in my fireplace.

Anca had laid another dress and a skirt on the counterpane, which had replaced the chenille bedspread. She had brought an oil lamp with her and had also lit the candles on the table by the side of my bed.

"Ah, good. I need to fit you for these."

Anca had her sewing box open on the floor and a pin cushion in her hand. She eyed the garments on the bed as she continued to remove the pins from a skirt that she had finished altering.

I sat before the fire, toweling my hair dry in its warmth. Tonight I would wear the black silk dress.

Grace barged into my room without knocking, shattering the equanimity that had settled around Anca and me. She was dressed in a bathrobe as well, but where mine was fuzzy and comfortable, hers was made of silk and trimmed with feathers. Her face, devoid of makeup, had hardened into an alabaster mask.

Her pale mouth, pinched and puckered in anger, just accentuated the hot fury in her eyes. "You haven't pulled the curtains to," she snapped at Anca. "We can't light the lamps until the curtains are shut. Surely you don't expect

Jack and me to do your job for you. How do you expect us to function in the dark?"

"I cannot do everything, madam."

"Of course, you can't do everything," Grace said. "But I have asked you repeatedly to shut the curtains at five o'clock, sharp."

I stood up and moved between Grace and Anca. "You can close a curtain or two, Grace. Anca's doing the work of four people all by herself."

"Anca is neglecting her duties to care for you. I find myself doing more around this house than both of you put together. All I'm asking for is a little help."

I almost apologized to Grace and let Anca go and do her mistress's bidding, but I had grown tired of the way Grace treated Anca and couldn't keep quiet any longer. "Caring for me is Anca's duty. She is my maid. You can check with my father if you don't believe me." I cringed at my choice of words. I had never referred to Anca as a servant or a maid. To me she was family.

Grace didn't know what to say to that. She opened her mouth to speak, thought better of it, and didn't say anything. Her eyes traveled to the garments on my bed. "What are those?" She reached to pick up the black wool skirt that Anca had just finished hemming.

I swooped in ahead of her, picked up the skirt, and draped it over my arm. "Those are my clothes."

Grace scrutinized the dresses and skirts laid out on the bed. "I don't remember packing up these things." Her words didn't hide the implication that clothes this fine would have wound up in her closet.

"I packed Sarah's things away myself." Anca stood up straight as she addressed Grace. She threw her proud Roma shoulders back. "I care for Miss Sarah's finest clothes."

"Do you think I might wear my mother's pearls?" I asked. "I noticed you had them. I assume you've been keeping them for me, and I'd like to wear them tonight."

Grace didn't argue. She looked at me with surprise, not quite sure which tone to strike. Finally, she forced a smile. "Of course, you can have them. If Anca will come with me, I will give them to her."

"No need. Anca has other things to do. I'll come with you and get them now."

"As you wish."

I followed Grace into the hall.

"I hope you don't think that Zeke is innocent just because he managed to get out of jail."

We had reached the door to her bedroom. I was surprised when she pulled a key out of the pocket of her robe and unlocked the door.

"He's not a spy, Grace. Just leave it alone, will you?"

"Wait here." She went into her bedroom, closing the door behind her. After a few seconds, she opened it again, thrusting the pearls at me. Her eyes never met mine.

"Thanks."

Grace didn't hear me. She had already slammed the door.

A line had been drawn between Grace and me. She was my father's wife and, as such, was the mistress of Bennett House. When I defended Anca and demanded my pearls, I had crossed that line. I hoped Anca wouldn't be the one to suffer the consequences.

Back in my room, Anca left my mended garments on the bed. I assumed she had gone down stairs to see to— one could only hope—closing the curtains and preparing dinner. I dressed myself, managing as best I could with one hand, trying to make my shaggy hair look presentable and wishing for some new make-up. I opened my last pair of silk stockings, grateful once again that Anca had hidden them away from Grace. I somehow managed to pin my hair up, and although it looked passable from the front, I had no idea what the back looked like and hoped that the hairpins I had used to hold the style in place weren't sticking out randomly. I pinched my cheeks to give myself some color and headed downstairs.

છ૭છ૭

The blackout curtains were pulled. The ferns that graced the fireplace when I first arrived had been re-moved. Now a fire burned brightly, but the room was still cold. From now until May, long sleeves would be re-quired in Bennett House. One could get warm by staying near the fire, but the rooms were too big, the ceilings too high in the old house for the fire to heat the rooms thoroughly. On the drinks trolley, an open bottle of champagne sat on ice. I poured myself a glass and walked over to the fire.

"You look absolutely fabulous, darling," Grace said as she glided over to me and planted a kiss on my cheek. She had on the blue dress again, but she hadn't bathed, which surprised me. Her hair was dirty, its greasy roots noticeable because of the tight chignon in which she wore it.

As she came over with the champagne bottle, she said, "Here, let me top off your glass." I smelled booze on her breath. It seemed as though my darling stepmother had started a little early.

I wanted to ask her what she had been doing for the past hour, for she hadn't been taking pains with her appearance. I was suspicious of her sudden change in attitude and had every intention of keeping my distance. Zeke came in looking gorgeous, despite the cuts and bruises on his face. He smiled at both of us as he picked up the champagne bottle, but decided against it, instead opting for a dollop of single-malt in one of the Waterford highball glasses that had been in the Bennett family for over a century. The crystal glass looked right in his hands. He swirled the glass a couple of times, but did not drink. He turned around and saw me standing before the fire.

I hoped Grace wouldn't notice the way Zeke and I looked at each other. No such luck. She sat curled up on the settee in the corner, sipped her drink, and watched us with a smug look on her face.

Zeke walked over to the sofa and we sat down next to each other.

"How do you like working for my father?" I asked.

"We haven't done much actual writing yet. We spend a lot of time discussing plot lines and characters, and I make some trips to the post office," he said. "Most of my time is spent scheduling book signings and speaking engagements. I've never had this sort of job before."

"How on earth did you manage to get hired?" Grace piped in. "I thought Jack would be more discerning than that."

"I'm afraid he might've felt sorry for me," Zeke said.

The front door opened and slammed shut. Footsteps clicked on the wooden floor. Gran burst into the room, her face red with fury. She didn't speak. She marched to the drinks trolley, poured herself a scotch, drank it in one go, and poured another. Zeke, Grace, and I stared at her in silence.

I had never seen her take more than a sip or two of champagne. She took her drink back to the couch and sat down.

I moved next to her and took her hand in mine. "What's happened? What's wrong?"

"I don't want to talk about it, Sarah Jane." She shook

my hand away. "Everything will be fine. I just need to speak to your father." She stood up.

"Jack's not here, Patricia. He had a last minute speaking engagement in Atherton at some women's club. Can I help you?" Grace asked.

"Absolutely not," Gran snapped. She turned her back on Grace and lowered her voice when she spoke to me. "Sarah, send him to me when he gets home. It is imperative that I speak to him immediately. He must come to my house, tonight."

I had no idea why Gran would entrust me, rather than Grace, with such a message. But I agreed to relay it.

"I must go. Sarah, don't forget. It's important."

"I won't. Are you not staying for dinner?"

"I've no appetite." She finished her scotch, set her drink down, and left the room without saying goodbye to anyone.

After she was gone, Grace stood up and left the room without a word.

"That was awkward." Zeke poured himself another drink. He came over with the champagne and poured some in my glass.

Anca came in to say that dinner was ready, and since Grace had gone up to her room and my father wasn't home, we dispensed with the formality of Anca serving at table, opting instead to eat in the kitchen. Before we ate, I slipped into my father's office and left him a note about Gran's earlier visit and her urgent need to see him.

We served ourselves and feasted on vegetable soufflé and tomato soup, along with crusty bread and fresh butter from the Bennett Cove dairy, all by the light of an oil lamp.

Anca regaled us with stories of her family in Romania. Her brother—so she claimed—was the finest horse trainer in the world. "My brother, he could get a horse to do anything. He even taught one how to pick pockets."

Her sister apparently was a fine musician and could play the fiddle better than any man. She told us about her family's gypsy lifestyle, traveling from place to place in their *vardo*—what we would call a covered wagon, and setting up their encampment along the countryside.

After we finished dinner and Anca started clearing the plates, Zeke excused himself, saying that he needed to take care of a few things for my father.

"He is falling in love with you." Anca washed the dishes while I finished clearing the table.

My heart beat faster. I couldn't bring myself to meet Anca's eyes.

"But that is a good thing, no? You have feelings, too.

"I don't know," I whispered.

Anca set the dish towel she was using down on the counter and came over to me. She put her hands on my shoulders, and looked at me, forcing me to meet her eyes. "You are a beautiful, intelligent woman. You deserve a loving husband just as much as anyone else."

"But what about my past? Should I tell him that I may have—"

"No. You did not push your mother down those stairs." Anca made the sign of the cross over her heart. "You get to know this man, when you trust him, you share your truth. If he is good, your past won't matter." Anca nodded, picked up the dish and said with finality, "He will love you for who you are."

I wish I had her confidence.

Our kitchen was a spacious room, designed for feeding and entertaining large parties. Off the kitchen was a long corridor which led to Anca's room, the washing machine, and the servant's staircase. The whole area was shrouded in shadow, as it is only lit with one overhead electric light, which was useless now that the storm had taken out the power. A long row of hooks graced the walls, holding the bulk of our raingear, warm coats, and hats. Below the hooks, a row of ancient Wellingtons in all sizes stood lined up, along with Anca's shopping bags and the linen basket. Grace's camera bag sat closest to the staircase.

I had just put the silver away, and was in the process of laying the used dish towels near the stove so they could dry overnight, when I saw Zeke in the back corridor. Something stopped me from speaking to him or asking what he was doing back here. He must have gone upstairs and come back down again on the servant's staircase, which no one ever used except Anca and me.

I ducked behind a huge parka and watched as Zeke bent over Grace's camera bag, unzipped it, and slipped out a black canister of film, all in one quick fluid motion. After he did that, he took another canister of film out of his pocket and slipped that into the camera bag in place of the film he had taken. He didn't see me standing in the shadows, spying on him. He headed back up the stairs, his footsteps quiet as passing time.

I walked back into the foyer and up the main staircase to my own room. Once inside, I locked the door behind me. I changed out of the black dress, fumbling with one hand. The image of Zeke switching the film in Grace's camera bag ran over and over in my head. I tried to convince myself that he hadn't been doing anything harmful. Maybe he just needed to borrow some film. But I knew what I had seen. I knew what I had heard this afternoon—Zeke speaking flawless German on the telephone.

The magic I had felt earlier, the possibility of a future with him had been clouded now. Our future together wouldn't be a happy one. How could it be? I had fallen in love with a spy.

# CHAPTER 7

The fire in my bedroom diminished during dinner, leaving my room as frigid as if there were no fire at all. I did nothing to warm it. Instead, I opened the window, letting the bracing sea air flood the room. Under cover of darkness, I changed into the thick corduroy trousers that I used for gardening. I put on a fisherman's sweater with a hood over a wool turtleneck. Then, so bundled, I lay down on the bed and settled in to wait. My father came home, and soon the bedroom doors near mine opened and shut for the night as Zeke, Grace, and, finally, my father readied for bed. I figured he had found the note I left him; whether or not he contacted Gran tonight was his business.

The house fell silent. Outside the owls hooted. Bennett House slept. I lay on my bed, trying to stay awake.

I awoke with a start to the sound of the deadbolt un-latching and the front door opening with a familiar creak of the ancient hinges. I got out of bed and stood on the chair by my window, craning my neck just in time to see a figure step out the door, into the front yard. Whoever it was had on dark trousers, a long dark coat, and a hat pulled low over his face, a disguise which would allow them to move about unseen in the cover of darkness. I watched as the figure headed to the mountain trail. I grabbed the gloves from my nightstand, hurried down the servant's staircase, and let myself out the kitchen door into the darkness of night. Using the high bushes near the house for cover, I followed the figure as he slipped into the dense woods at the base of the mountain.

We trekked along the trails that wove up the moun-tainside. Whoever I followed moved quickly, with knowledge of these trails that impressed, forcing me to work hard to stay out of sight. My breathing became la-bored, but I remained undetected as I followed the person up the narrow trail onto the dirt road.

When the distant hum of an approaching car broke the still night, the person who I followed moved into the shadows. The car approached. Only a fool would drive at night without headlights on this dangerous road. One false move and the car would tumble hundreds of feet down the face of rocky cliffs into the ocean below. I peered out from the bushes and saw a dark, nondescript

car, a Chevy or a Studebaker—I couldn't tell in the darkness—approaching at a slow crawl. The car came to a
stop and flashed its headlights, twice, before it turned
them off again. The person I had followed—I had to face
the fact that, in all likelihood, I followed Zeke—stepped
out of the shadows and got into the passenger seat. Keeping the headlights off, the car pulled onto the narrow dirt
shoulder, turned around, and drove away. I could not follow the car on foot, so I turned back and took the road
home, no longer worried about staying out of sight, no
closer to the truth about Zeke than I had been earlier.

By the time I arrived back at Bennett House, my
hands and feet were numb with cold. I slipped in through
the front door, surprised to see firelight come from the
library.

My father was still awake. He sat in his winged chair
before the blaze, holding a picture of my dead mother in
his lap. He didn't hear me come in, and was oblivious to
my presence as I stood watching him from the doorjamb.
I had been so preoccupied with my own problems I
hadn't noticed the gray hair that used to be at his temples
had now taken root everywhere.

His hands, which held a picture of my mother, had
noticeable age spots. They had become the hands of a
man at the tail end of middle age.

I coughed so he would know I was there, and by the
time I had stepped into the room, the picture of my dead
mother had been tucked out of sight.

"What are you doing up so late?" he asked.

I pulled the ottoman that rested beside the fireplace up close to his chair and sat down. "I need to talk to you." I explained how I had followed the masked figure out the front door and about the rendezvous with the car. "He got in and drove away."

He stared at his glass and swirled the amber liquid that glistened in the firelight. "Do you think it was Zeke?"

I nodded, fearing that the simple act of uttering the words would open the floodgate that held my emotions at bay. My father set his drink down on the table and stood. He walked over to the fire, and held his hands out for its warmth.

"What are we going to do?" The tears I had almost shed were gone now, pulled in and galvanized into a hard lump in the back of my throat.

"We are not going to do anything." He turned around to face me. "I'm going to call Colonel Matthews tomorrow. If someone in this household is a spy, they must be stopped." My father refilled his glass from the crystal decanter. "I know I don't do a very good job of showing it, but I'm glad you're home, Sarah. I'm hopeful that you will remember what happened the night your mother died, if only so you can have some peace in your life."

"Thank you."

"I'll do anything to help you, Sarah. You know that, don't you?"

I nodded. "You got my note? Gran was quite anxious to speak to you."

"She's fine now. We sorted everything out."

"I'm going up to bed. I'll see you in the morning." I stood up, squeezed my father's shoulder, and headed out of the room

It wasn't until I had closed my bedroom window, pulled the curtains, and stoked the fire that exhaustion set in. I changed into my warm flannel pajamas and got under the covers, but alas, sleep didn't come.

Zeke plagued my thoughts and kept me awake. I tossed and turned until the covers were knotted around my ankles. I got up, straightened the bed, and tried once again to fall asleep.

I turned on my side, couldn't get comfortable, so I flipped to my other side and tried putting an extra pillow between my knees. My mind raced. I would start to fall asleep, until images of Zeke with a noose around his neck floated through my head.

I dozed off, only to be jolted awake by loud shouting. The tortured cries came from down the hall.

I got up and pulled my robe on, tying the sash around my waist as I headed toward the source of the screaming. My father's bedroom door opened as I hurried past it, and he joined me in the hall, his wool bathrobe hanging loose and unbelted over his street clothes.

"What in God's name is that racket?" We stopped outside of Zeke's room. My father pounded the wooden door with his fist. "Zeke, open up. What's wrong, man?" He pounded on the door again.

The screams had morphed into groans, then into a pathetic whimpering before it stopped altogether. The hallway was silent for a moment. My father and I looked at each other, waiting to see if the nightmares had ceased. They hadn't. The whimpering started again, followed by shouting, this time louder than before.

"William," Zeke screamed.

"Do something."

"Move away from the door."

I stepped out of his way. In a surprising show of strength, he stepped back and charged the door with all his might. The heavy door didn't budge. The screaming on the other side of it became louder. Fully awake now, my father, rubbing his shoulder, reached down into a holster that he had hidden under the leg of his trousers. He pulled out a gun.

He didn't have to tell me to cover my ears. I moved far back and stuck my fingers in them. He pulled the trigger, but nothing happened.

"What's wrong?"

"It's jammed." He took the bullets out and reloaded. He aimed and fired once again. This time the bullet discharged and the lock shattered. The shouting had stopped. The only sound was the door as it swung open on squeaky hinges. We entered Zeke's room. My father struck a match and lit the oil lamp that sat atop the old rosewood dresser. The door to Zeke's wardrobe was open, revealing three suits, a camel hair overcoat, two fedoras, and three pairs of shoes, all neatly arranged. The right side had rows for shirts and collar stays.

There was no sign of the dark clothing that he had worn earlier, if indeed it was Zeke I had seen having a rendezvous in the middle of the night.

He lay on his bed on his side, his knees drawn up to his chest. His covers lay on the floor in a tangled mess. His skin glistened with sweat. His eyes were open, but they were glassy with fever. He whimpered, oblivious to our presence.

My father went over to the bed. I went after him, pushed him aside, and sat down on the bed next to Zeke.

I reached out and placed my hand on his shoulder. His skin was hot with fever, slick with sweat.

"No," he cried out, cowering at my touch.

"Zeke, it's me, Sarah." I didn't take my hand away.

He closed his eyes and seemed to slip into unconsciousness. I sensed Anca standing in the doorway.

"Tea and brandy, please, Anca," my father ordered.

She made the motion of the cross, offering Zeke a silent blessing before she left us.

I rubbed his shoulder. "Zeke?"

His breathing, which had been ragged and sharp, slowed a bit. He shook his head from side to side, as if to clear the thoughts that haunted him. When he opened his eyes, they were filled with tears.

He looked so pale that I wondered if he was going to die. "Sarah," he whispered.

"I'm here."

"You need to get out of here. It is not safe." It seemed as if speaking the words took all of his energy. His eyes started to close. "I love you," he whispered.

My face grew hot. I didn't dare look at my father. He stepped close to Zeke. I moved aside to let him sit down on the bed. He placed his hand on Zeke's shoulder where mine had been and gently shook him. "Wake up, young man."

When Zeke opened his eyes this time, he knew where he was. He looked around the room, at my father, then at me. He pulled himself up to a sitting position and ran his hand over his face, while his eyes frantically traveled around the room until they landed on the attaché case that was tucked near the wall next to his dresser. "Did I wake you both up?"

He went to pull the blankets over him, but couldn't reach them without getting up. My father picked them up and covered Zeke.

Anca came in with the tea and brandy. She poured a generous dollop in Zeke's teacup before she handed it to him. "Drink this. You need soup. I will go get a tray."

"That's all right. Don't go to any trouble on my behalf."

"You need soup," she said, leaving us once again.

"This is embarrassing," Zeke said. He swallowed the

brandy-laced tea in one swig, tipping the delicate cup back and draining it. Soon the color started to come back into his cheeks. "I've been having these nightmares for some time."

"We heard you shouting. It woke us," I said.

"I had to shoot the door down." My father examined the damage to the lock. "This will have to be replaced." He looked at Zeke. "I'm afraid you won't be able to lock your door."

Soon Anca came back with a tray carrying a bowl of hot chicken noodle soup and homemade bread.

"Thank you, Anca," Zeke said as Anca laid the tray on his lap.

"You're a good boy." Anca smiled at Zeke before she shot me a knowing glance.

"I owe you both an explanation," Zeke said, looking at my father and me.

"You owe us nothing," my father said. "What happened to you before you came here is your business. I imagine it's quite painful. Sarah and I certainly don't need you to rehash your suffering and loss to satisfy our curiosity. Come on, Sarah, let's leave Zeke alone."

"Thanks for coming to my rescue. Sorry to cause such a disturbance in the middle of the night," Zeke said.

"We'll talk in the morning," my father said. "Good night."

Once we were out in the corridor, my father looked at me strangely.

"You seem to have made quite an impression on Zeke."

I didn't know what to say to that.

"Don't take the things he said too seriously, Sarah. His mind was wandering. For all we know, he could have been professing his love to someone else entirely."

"You don't approve of Zeke?"

"It's not that I don't approve of him, I just don't want you to get hurt. Not now, not after everything you've been through. Especially since this young man's actions of late have been suspicious."

We were standing in front of Grace's room.

"I'm surprised that Grace didn't wake up," I said.

"She probably took a sleeping powder. She would sleep through an invasion."

"Let's hope it doesn't come to that," I said.

He smiled at me, went into his room, and shut the door behind him.

It wasn't until after the door clicked shut and the lock slid home that I realized I had neglected to ask my father what on earth he was doing with a gun in an ankle holster hidden under the leg of his trousers.

# CHAPTER 8

Anca woke me up the next morning when she came in the room carrying a tray laden with tea and fresh baked scones.

She placed the tray on my dresser and walked over to the window, where she whipped open the curtains in one noisy swoosh.

I sat up and rubbed my eyes. "I'm awake."

The sound of spraying gravel and screeching brakes announced the car that skidded to a halt within inches of the steps that lead to the front porch. I got out of bed and pulled the chair up to my window, where I hoisted myself up and perched my elbows against the sill, craning my neck to see the activity in the driveway below.

Sheriff Carpenter got out of the car and shuffled toward the front door, one hand resting on his lower back.

"Didn't Sheriff Carpenter retire?"

"He did, but the young man who took his place signed up to fight, so he had to come back to work." Anca stood next to me on her tip toes, peering out the window into the driveway below.

Sheriff Carpenter waited near his car as another car pulled up behind his. A deputy got out—a young man who looked as though he could still be in high school—along with Colonel Matthews. Both men followed Sheriff Carpenter up to the front door.

My stepmother opened the front door before they had a chance to knock. "Yes?"

I couldn't hear what Sheriff Carpenter said in return, but the men came into the house, and soon the murmur of their voices could be heard through my open bedroom door.

I splashed water on my face, pulled my hair back, secured it with a clip, and headed downstairs, only to find the door to my father's office closed. I put my ear against it, trying to make sense of the low mumble of words on the other side.

Sheriff Carpenter said something that I couldn't make out, but when Colonel Matthews spoke, his voice was loud enough for me to hear his words clearly. "Do you think Sarah is stable? She's never shown any inclination toward violence, has she, Jack?"

"I can't make any guarantees about Sarah's emotional state. She had a rough time when Jessica died, but no, Sarah has never been violent."

"Oh, here she is." Grace opened the door before I could pull my ear away. "Were you eavesdropping, Sarah?" She spoke in a whisper so the men couldn't hear. "You could have just come in." She looked glamorous in a straight black skirt and a crisp white blouse. Her hair was pulled back into a chignon, showing off her long graceful neck. "The sheriff would like to speak with you." She stepped aside and held the door open for me.

Despite the warm fire in the hearth and the golden morning sun that came through the leaded windows in my father's office, the mood when I walked in the room was frosty at best. Grace followed behind me. After she shut the door, she took her position behind my father, like a queen standing behind her enthroned king. In the unforgiving morning sunlight, I could see that despite Grace's polished ensemble, her face was drawn and pale, her mouth pinched into a tight line. The circles under her eyes belied the deep sleep that she got last night, a sleep so deep that she didn't awaken when my father fired his gun at Zeke's bedroom door.

Colonel Matthews stood against the wall near the desk, his hands clasped in front of him in a perfect parade rest. He didn't smile at me when I came into the room. No one did. The young deputy stood next to Colonel Matthews, but looked like a young and fidgety colt next to the colonel's staid bearing. The young deputy cast his eyes my way, and when I nodded at him, he blushed crimson and riveted his eyes on his feet. Sheriff Carpenter sat in the guest chair in front of my father's desk.

Zeke sat at his own desk. A neat stack of papers lay before him, but he had pushed them aside. He looked horrible. His green eyes were rimmed in red, the shadows under them dark against his pale skin. The stitches on his cheek added to his haggard appearance. A small drop of blood had congealed along the strong line of his jaw where he had cut himself shaving. He gave me a nod and returned his focus to the group gathered at my father's desk.

"Good morning." I spoke to Zeke in a soft voice that only he could hear. "Are you okay?"

"Much better, thanks." He gave me a wistful smile before he looked away.

I knew Sheriff Carpenter to be a fair, honest man, who cared deeply about Bennett Cove and the people who lived here. He had been the only law enforcement officer in town for as long as I could remember. I had fond childhood memories of Sheriff Carpenter at Christmastime, dressing up as Santa Claus and sitting under the big Christmas tree in town, kindly listening to the Christmas wishes of Bennett Cove's children.

"Sarah, here you are." My father got up from his desk and went to stand near Colonel Matthews. He nodded at Sheriff Carpenter, who took the seat behind my father's desk.

"Have a seat, Sarah," Sheriff Carpenter said, beckoning to the empty chair.

I could no more open my mouth and speak than I could fly to the moon. I approached the desk, as if in slow motion, bracing myself for what was to come.

"We've had some bad news," my father said finally, his voice breaking. His eyes filled with tears, but he quickly wiped them away with the back of his hand.

"Your grandmother has been found—" Sheriff Carpenter couldn't finish his sentence.

My father spoke, filling in the vacuous silence. "Colonel Matthews's men found her down by the beach."

"What?" My voice was a whisper.

Grace came from around the desk and grabbed my hand. "I'm so sorry. I know you and Patricia were close."

"I don't understand. What are you talking about?"

"Sarah, your grandmother has been murdered," Zeke said. He came over and sat in the chair next to me. He didn't touch me, but the physical nearness of him gave me strength.

"She was killed sometime last night," Sheriff Carpenter said. "Jack, you'll need to come and identify the body." He stood up, surprisingly tall in spite of his aged stoop. "But first, I would like to speak with each of you individually. This is how it works. I'll be conducting short interviews right now. After we evaluate, I'll want to speak with everyone at length, so you need to be available."

"Surely you don't think one of us killed her," my father said.

"This is a serious matter, Jack. Everyone is a suspect," Sheriff Carpenter said. He nodded at Colonel Matthews, who had been silent until now.

"We have a theory," Colonel Matthews interjected. He stepped out of the corner and, in the way of a man who is accustomed to giving orders, took command. "Everyone in this room knows that there is a cordoned-off section of the beach, where we've built what looks like an old farmhouse and barn. I cannot tell you what we are doing there, but I will tell you that someone tried to sabotage the building last night with an incendiary bomb. Luckily, we found the device and were able to disarm it without any injury or damage. This isn't the first time that someone has tried to sabotage my operation, but last night they almost succeeded.

"It's possible that Patricia interrupted someone or saw something when she was out on one of her walks. She does have a tendency to tromp through the woods, and although I mean no disrespect, she does have an uncanny knack for putting her nose into other people's business."

"You think the sabotage at your facility is related to Patricia's murder?" Zeke asked.

Colonel Matthews gave him a shut-up-and-listen look.

"Well, do you?" Zeke pushed.

Colonel Matthews ignored him. "One of my men saw a person disguised in dark clothing sneaking around the other night. We gave chase, but they slipped into the woods and got away. It stands to reason that Patricia might have seen something." Colonel Matthews stopped speaking, as if checking himself, making sure he didn't reveal too much. He paused and looked around the room, engaging each and every one of us. "Let's just say there are significant unanswered questions."

"So now you're suggesting my mother-in-law was a spy?" My father's voice had a flinty edge to it.

"She may have seen something, that's all I'm saying," Colonel Matthews said. "Out of respect for you and your family, I'm telling you where things stand."

Gran was dead. I couldn't take it in, couldn't process it. My father reached for the cup of coffee on his desk, but his hand shook so much, that he set it back down again.

"I'll identify her, Jack, if you would like," Zeke said.

"No," my father said. "It's my responsibility."

"If you ladies will excuse us," Sheriff Carpenter said. He herded Grace and me out of the room and shut the door behind us.

"I'm not really sure why we had to leave the room," I said to Grace.

As we headed towards the kitchen, I wondered why it was that whenever crisis struck, food must be prepared. Was the act of preparation a panacea for the preparers, or did everyone really get hungry in times of tragedy?

"They probably thought the details were too much for us." Grace stopped and grabbed my hand. "I'm sorry, Sarah. That was thoughtless of me." Light came in through windows, shining on the old chopping block in the middle of the kitchen.

"It's just so hard to believe that Gran is dead. I just saw her yesterday."

Neither one of us spoke as we made coffee, a pot of tea, and put the rest of Anca's scones on a plate.

"We should probably make sandwiches, too." Grace had opened the cupboard and was surveying our food supply.

"With what?"

"Bread and butter," she said. "I'll see to it."

I left Grace making the sandwiches while I took the tea tray and scones into my father's office. I went in without knocking, plowing right into the middle of a heated argument between Colonel Matthews and Zeke.

"She's not—" Zeke said. When I walked into the room, he stopped talking.

Everyone stopped what they were doing and remained still and silent, until I deposited the tray on Zeke's desk—the only clear spot in the room. That completed, I saw myself out of the office. By the time I joined Grace in the drawing room, a cold knot had formed in my belly. I had half a mind to build a fire, but couldn't find the energy to rouse myself from the couch.

"It's freezing in here. Shall I build a fire?" Grace sat next to me, her shoes kicked off on the floor, her legs tucked under her.

"If you like," I said. "I'm surprised we didn't wake you last night."

"Why? What happened?"

"Zeke had a horrible nightmare. The door was locked, so my father had to shoot the door open."

"I take a strong sleeping powder," Grace said. "I suffer from horrible insomnia."

"Well, I'm glad that we didn't—"

The young red-headed deputy came into the room.

"Miss Grace, Sheriff Carpenter is ready for you."

"We'll talk later." Grace smiled at me as she followed the deputy toward the office.

My father came in just as Grace was leaving. When they passed near each other, Grace gently touched his arm. He pushed her hand away. For the most part, my father was an affable, social creature, but he did have his moods and would withdraw behind his stoic, unflappable fortress.

I pitied Grace. How awful to have a husband, the man she loved, shut her out just when they needed each other most. Lucky for her, my father had been known to snap out of his moods just as quickly as they came over him.

Now he poured himself a finger of scotch, drank it, and poured another generous dollop, which he took to one of the winged chairs in front of the fireplace. He sat down, seemingly oblivious of my presence.

"Are you all right?"

"You mean aside from the fact that my mother-in-law has been murdered?" He put his hand over his face and rubbed his eyes. "I'm sorry, Sarah. I just can't believe it."

"I can't believe that Gran provoked someone to kill her."

"Really?" my father said.

"Whatever do you mean?" I asked.

"She was always sticking her nose into other people's business."

He stood and started to pace around the room, round and round he walked, as if I weren't there. The realization that Gran was gone for good sank in with a fatal finality. I sat back on the sofa, chilled to the bone and full of regret that I had left the cocoon of The Laurels and had come home to Bennett House.

"Her wedding ring is missing. Did they tell you that? Somebody murdered her for that diamond. I told her she shouldn't wear such a valuable ring when she went off walking by herself."

I didn't know what to say to him. I didn't know anything anymore.

The young deputy reappeared. "Miss Bennett?"

I stood and followed him back into my father's office. Grace was nowhere to be seen. Colonel Matthews sat in one of the chairs across from my father's desk. Zeke had been allowed to stay in the room, for some reason. He sat at his desk, with the chair still turned sideways. He crossed his legs and leaned back against the wall, a gesture that set him apart from the other men, as if to say he wasn't a part of their united front. He was his own person. He gave me a slight smile and an encouraging nod as I sat down in the chair opposite Sheriff Carpenter.

The sheriff got right to the point. "Tell me about your movements last night."

I explained as clearly as I could how I had wound up following the mysterious person up the trail. I told the sheriff everything, only leaving out that the person had come from Bennett House. I couldn't do that to Zeke—if he was the person I had seen out on the trail.

"So you just happened to be fully dressed in the middle of the night? You just happened to see a mysterious figure in the woods and you happened to follow them?" The sheriff didn't bother hiding the cynicism that had crept into his voice.

I met his eyes and didn't flinch or look away. "Yes."

Gone was the man who used to dress up like Santa Claus. This man, charged with solving my grandmother's murder, had a cold ruthlessness about him. He would get to the bottom of this. He would find out what happened to Gran. I hoped that Zeke would be hurt in the process.

The sheriff went back to his notebook, flipped

through the pages as if to check some facts from his previous interviews. He flipped forward and wrote in the notebook. After about ten minutes, he looked up at me again, searching my face. "Did you kill your grandmother?"

"Of course not," I snapped at him. "That's ridiculous."

"Everyone knows that your grandmother walks around these hills, knows the trails like the back of her hands. So do you."

"So do a lot of other people," Zeke said. "I don't like where you're going with this, Sheriff."

"He's just doing his job, son," Colonel Matthews said.

"I'm not your son," Zeke said.

The door opened and the young deputy came in. He shot me a look as he leaned over and whispered into the sheriff's ear. The sheriff stood.

"Stay where you are. I'll be back shortly." He followed the young deputy out of the room, leaving Zeke, Colonel Matthews, and I alone in the room.

"What's going on? Do they really think I killed her?"

"Probably not," Zeke said. "I think they just want to test you, you know, to see what your reaction is. He's got to be a little hardnosed. It's his job."

The sheriff and his deputy came back into the room. Sheriff Carpenter's face was mottled red. The vein that jagged across his forehead throbbed. He held my coat over one arm. In his other hand he held the wet shoes that I wore outside the night before. "Is this your coat, Miss Bennett?" he asked.

"Yes," I said.

He used his white handkerchief to extricate a bloody knife from the pocket of my coat. The knife was identical to the one I had discovered in the bottom drawer of my father's desk, only now the lethal blade was encrusted with a brown gooey material that I knew without asking was Gran's blood.

"Have you seen this knife before? Think carefully because we found it in your coat pocket." The sheriff dangled the knife in front of me.

"Yes," I said. "I found it in the bottom drawer of the desk. I took it out this morning. My father even commented on how strange it was because he had never seen it before." I looked imploringly at Zeke and Sheriff Carpenter. "I put it back."

"Which drawer," Sheriff Carpenter asked.

He let me come around beside him. I opened the center drawer, took out the old brass key and unlocked the drawer that held the ledgers and deeds. I took them all out, every one of them. There at the bottom of the drawer lay the knife.

"I don't understand," I said.

"Maybe there are two knives," the sheriff said. "This is the one with your fingerprints on it?" He pointed to the knife in the drawer.

I nodded, stepped out of the way, and sat back down in the chair opposite the desk.

He nodded at the young deputy who took the knife out of the drawer with a handkerchief and placed it on the desk next to the bloody one.

My heart pounded. The room spun. I concentrated on breathing, and prayed that I wouldn't pass out.

"I didn't kill her," I said, my voice sounding weak. I stood up, God only knows why. My knees certainly weren't capable of supporting my body weight. I plopped back down before they buckled beneath me.

"Tell me about your time at The Laurels." Sheriff Carpenter sat back down in my father's chair. The bloody knife lay on the desk between us.

Zeke jumped up from his desk and stood behind the chair where I sat. "Can't you see she's about to faint?" He put his hand on my shoulder. "Sarah, bend over, put your head down."

I did as he said, taking deep breaths in an effort to calm myself. When I sat back up, the dizziness had stopped. Sheriff Carpenter watched me, a suspicious gleam in his eye.

"Do you think Sarah would leave the murder weapon in her coat if she killed her grandmother? She's not stupid," Zeke said. "She doesn't have to tell you about her time away, either. Does she need a lawyer?"

"He has a point," Colonel Matthews said, "about the knife, anyway."

"This isn't the first unseemly death she's been involved with," Sheriff Carpenter said.

"That is out of line, sir, and you know it," Zeke said. "Don't you think she's suffered enough?"

Sheriff Carpenter looked at Zeke and at Colonel Matthews, their silent communication conveyed some secret to which I was not privy. I might have spent time in an asylum, but I did not kill Gran, and I was not going to be charged for her murder. I had nothing to hide.

"Am I going to find your fingerprints on this?" Sheriff Carpenter pointed to the unsullied knife that lay on the desk.

"Yes. As I told you, I touched it when I took it out of the drawer and again when I put it back."

The sheriff nodded to his deputy, who took both knives away.

"Who else has access to this drawer?" The sheriff asked.

"I imagine anyone," I said. "We leave the house unlocked. My father leaves his French doors open when the weather is fine. Anyone could come in here."

"I don't need to tell you not to leave town. Tell your father we'll be back this afternoon to continue our investigation. I'm sure we'll have more questions. Meanwhile, I'd appreciate it if you stayed away from your grandmother's home. We'll be conducting a search of the premises as soon as we are able."

He nodded at Zeke and Colonel Matthews who, in

turn, stood up and followed the sheriff to the door.

"This is going to sort itself out," Zeke said.

"They think I killed her," I said.

"I'm going to prove you didn't. I promise you that. I need to go with them. Will you be okay here?

I nodded.

After Zeke left, I stayed in the chair for a long time, numb, frightened, and overcome with a profound sense of foreboding.

# CHAPTER 9

I don't know how long I sat like that, alone in the office, lost in my own thoughts. Eventually my father came into the room, ignoring me as he sat in the chair behind his desk, fiddling with the papers that rested on top of it.

"They found a bloody knife in my coat pocket," I said.

My father stopped toying with the stack of unopened mail on his desk and stared at me.

"But surely they don't think you killed her. You have no motive. Someone must have planted the knife in your coat pocket."

"Who? Zeke, Anca, you, Grace? Why would anyone do that? It doesn't make sense."

I walked over to the window and stared out at the redwood trees beyond the grass.

"There is no way they are going to pin Gran's murder on you. You didn't do it. Anyone could have gotten in this house at any time. We've become a little more diligent, but we don't exactly lock down the house every night. I leave my French doors open all the time during the day. Everyone knows there are saboteurs in Bennett Cove. How do we know they didn't come in here, get the knife, and go after your grandmother? You know as well as I do, she walks all over the mountain. Who knows what she saw? If she saw someone acting suspiciously, I'm sure she wouldn't have slunk away. This person— whoever did this—is obviously a cunning, professional killer."

He sat down on the sofa, leaned back, and crossed his legs. He set his drink down on the coffee table before he stood up once again.

"This will be sorted out, Sarah. Meanwhile, I'm going to get a lawyer for you. You need to be protected. I'll see that things are handled."

"Do you think it will come to that? Surely they won't charge me with a crime if they've no proof."

"We can't let it go that far. Let me take care of this for you. Don't worry. I'll handle it." He jiggled the change in his pocket, nodded at me, and left the room.

I was a suspect in Gran's murder. My father's promise to get me a lawyer did little to assuage my angst.

എജ

The kitchen smelled of the chicken stock that boiled away on the stove. Anca and Mrs. Tolliver sat at the refectory table, the brown utilitarian tea pot between them, along with a plate of ginger cakes and a crock of jam that I recognized as Mrs. Tolliver's. A strange-looking flower arrangement in a blue Mason jar rested on the table in front of Mrs. Tolliver.

"Sarah needs to remember what happened that night." Anca didn't realize that I stood in the doorway, listening. "I know in my heart that she saw something."

"She does. That's the only way to set things right." Mrs. Tolliver reached over and squeezed Anca's hand. "Don't worry. She's going to be fine. Things will get worse before they get better, but in the end, the girl will be better off."

Anca made the sign of the cross over her bosom. "I'm so afraid."

"There she is." Mrs. Tolliver smiled at me as she slid the Mason jar full of flowers across the table toward me. "I brought you something. That's rosemary, chrysanthemum, blackberry vine, roses, and fennel, tied with a band of garlic that I braided myself."

"Thank you."

"The rosemary is for remembrance, everything else is for protection. You're going to need it. Keep that vase near your bed. It will help you."

"I'm just down for a hot water bottle." I did not want to hear Mrs. Tolliver's discourse about what my future held and how her magic could protect me. I had hoped that getting in bed under the covers with a hot water bottle would dispel the cold chill that enveloped my heart.

"I'll bring it up to you." Anca started to stand up.

"That's okay. I'll get it." I took the old tea kettle to the sink where I filled it up with water. I set it on the stove, and settled in to wait for it to boil.

"I must be getting on." Mrs. Tolliver stood up and put her coat on. "I've got days' worth of canning to do. Goodbye, Anca. Stay strong, Sarah. My door is open if you need me. And I'm sorry about your Gran." She headed out into the fall afternoon.

I filled the hot water bottle from the kettle on the stove and carried it, along with Mrs. Tolliver's flower arrangement, back up to my bedroom. I set the flowers next to my bed and laid down with a wool blanket over me and the hot water bottle against my stomach. I dozed. When I woke up, my hot water bottle had gone cold and bright beams of afternoon sun bathed my room in muted, yellow light.

I needed to get up, get moving, and do something physical. The shutter on the front of the house needed mending. The roses needed a major pruning. With a sense of purpose, I redressed the wound on my hand with a bandage that wasn't quite so bulky and headed downstairs. The house stood still and quiet. My father had locked himself in his study. Grace was nowhere to be seen. Anca had gone to town to place our weekly grocery order. I made myself a lunch of bread, cheese, and apples. I had just finished eating and was about to put on my rubber boots and go outside when Zeke burst in the front door.

I stood up and walked over to him. "What's the matter?"

He opened the leather satchel that he carried under his arm and pulled out a photograph and the portrait that I had drawn. He threw both of them on the empty table in the foyer.

"You took my picture," I said.

"You dropped it, so I kept it."

I tried to snatch the picture, but Zeke grabbed it first. He arranged both pictures on the table so they lay side by side, facing me. I stared at the sketch, drawn in my hand, the sketch that I didn't remember drawing. I had never undertaken a portrait and was once again surprised at my own prowess. I had captured Mrs. Kensington's essence, as though I could blink my eyes and her image would come to life.

My eyes traveled to the eight-by-ten photograph that Zeke had placed on the table next to my sketch. Mrs. Kensington stared up at me from the photo and the sketch I had drawn. The images were identical. Zeke watched me warily as I scrutinized both images. How could I explain to him that I didn't remember drawing the picture and couldn't replicate the effort if my life depended on it?

From the style of Mrs. Kensington's hair and the age of the picture, I would guess that it was taken about twenty years ago. She had on a fitted black dress with sheer fabric covering her shoulders and her décolleté. The familiar locket hung from a fine chain around her neck, resting in the hollow below her throat. She had smiled for her portrait, the smile of a woman who experienced the world in a loving way.

"I drew a picture, okay?" I said. I snatched the picture that I had drawn and tore it up.

"Sarah," he said, his voice softening, "this is very important. I need you to think. I need you to remember and tell me exactly when you saw this woman. Are you sure she was here in Bennett Cove?"

"I told you I met her while I was away. Her daughter was staying at the same place. Mrs. Kensington and I met in the library and struck up a friendship. I don't usually draw portraits. I usually draw flowers—I—"

Zeke gripped my arm and led me out the front door. He didn't speak, just herded me away from the house and toward the ocean. When we reached the beach, he let go of my arm.

"I need you to assure me that you really did see this woman," he said.

"I told you the truth," I said, pulling away from him. I rubbed my elbow where he had clenched it. "I met her at The Laurels. She came to see her daughter and we struck up an acquaintance." I recalled the day we met on the beach, my surprise that Grace Kensington had followed me to Bennett Cove.

"What? What are you remembering?" Zeke asked.

I told him of our meeting on the beach.

"She was certain that I didn't kill my mother," I said. "At first I thought she was a reporter, lying to get a story. Why are you asking anyway? Who is she to you?"

Zeke gazed out at the ocean. He weighed his words before he spoke. "I was hired to find her, but I was sent here without a picture. Imagine my surprise when I opened the envelope I received today and saw this." He took the picture out of his pocket and waved it at me.

"Well, that shouldn't be too difficult. She's here in Bennett Cove," I said.

"Sarah, she perished in a fire over a year ago," Zeke said. "It took a while for the coroner to identify her because we had to wait for her dental records from Maine. Her dentist enlisted, so it took longer than usual. This woman is dead."

Stars burst behind my eyes. My knees gave out, and I would have fallen had Zeke not steadied me. I thought back to an evening at the Laurels, when Mrs. Kensington and I had sat together in the library and had a long conversation about *Rebecca* by Daphne du Maurier. On that day, she had declined the tea I offered, but we had sat together in the window seat overlooking the San Francisco Bay. Mrs. Kensington had told me about Cornwall, where

Daphne du Maurier wrote many of her books. We had a lovely visit. After Mrs. Kensington had left, the nurse had come in to give me medicine and tend to me in my room. I had asked her about the elegant and kind-hearted woman, who took time away from her daughter to visit me, a lonely stranger, a long way from home, but the nurse had changed the subject so quickly, I had laughed out loud at her utter lack of subtlety. The nurse had looked at me as though I were seeing things. Now I knew why.

"Do you want to tell me what happened to your hand?" Zeke asked. He took my hand and kissed it, his lips hot on my skin. He turned my palm up and gently removed the simple bandage that covered the burn, revealing the scar from my dream.

"You're not going to believe it."

I told Zeke everything. I told him of the vivid dream I had, of the fire, and the searing pain in my hand that I had brought with me from slumber.

I reckoned he deserved the truth, and I hoped at some point he would reciprocate in kind and be truthful with me about his life, about the horrors that caused his nightmares. When I finished speaking, Zeke wrapped his arms around me, encircling me with warmth. I savored the heat of him, the musky smell that made my senses reel.

"Has anything like this ever happened to you before?" His voice was soft in my ear, his breath hot against my neck.

I shrugged. "When I was a child, I had a few imaginary friends, but all children have those."

"I was sent here to find the real Grace Kensington," Zeke said. "Unfortunately, I didn't get her picture until today. When I opened that envelope and found an exact replica of the portrait you drew, I didn't know what to think."

I leaned into him, not the least bit ashamed of my desire to be close to him. I let the strength of his body hold me up. His chin rested on the top of my head. I leaned away from him and met his eyes. When our lips met, I didn't resist. Our kiss was long and deep, and when it ended, we clung to each other, our bodies pressed together in the October sun.

"My great grandmother could see the souls of those who had crossed," he whispered in my ear. "People in my small town were afraid of her. It wasn't something she talked about much. Better to keep something like that quiet. Most people don't understand."

"Tell me why you switched the film in my stepmother's camera bag."

"You saw that?" Zeke smiled and shook his head. "I sensed someone watching me. No wonder you've been suspicious of me."

"You're German is so fluent. Are you a—"

"Spy?" He finished my question. "I suppose so. But I work for the Federal Bureau of Investigation. I speak French and Italian too. My language skills are an asset.

We are pursuing a group of Nazi sympathizers who have stolen plans for ships and planes. We have tried to intercept communiques with little success. They have gotten stronger and more sophisticated lately."

"So you know who the spy is?" I asked.

"Yes," he said. "But we don't have much proof. Our aim is to discover for whom she works. As far as we know, she could just be a courier or a high-level operative disguised as such. We have intelligence that she could be working for an entire network operating along the California coast."

"She?" I asked.

Zeke paused for a moment before he spoke. What a deliberate man he was, I thought. He never spoke without thinking. What I wouldn't give to be blessed with that kind of a mind. Finally, he looked down at me. I shivered as he ran his index finger across my upper lip, surprised that a gesture so simple could elicit such waves of pleasure. "It's your stepmother," Zeke said. "Personally, I am convinced she is a spy, a saboteur, and a murderer. As soon as I can find out who she is working with, she'll be arrested. By the grace of God, she'll swing for treason."

He took my hand and led me up to the dunes, where we would be protected from the wind that whipped up around us. As we sat next to each other, Zeke put his arm around me, sheltering me from the wind.

"About two years ago," Zeke said, "a woman, who went by the name of Vicky Michaels, worked as a secretary at Hamilton Air Force Base. She ingratiated herself with the top-ranking men, and, before too long, she had access to so much information it doesn't bear thinking about. It is believed she took photos of classified documents and passed them along to the German factions that are here in the United States.

"A sting operation was set up in the hopes of catching her, but she had contacts who knew of the sting. On the day she was scheduled to be arrested, she disappeared. Then she resurfaced under the name Vivian Mason and took a job caring for an elderly lady, a Joyce Kensington, in San Francisco. The FBI was ready to sweep in and arrest her when she was allegedly killed, along with the elderly woman that she cared for, in a fire. We've reason to believe that Vivian didn't die in the fire, but that a woman named Grace Kensington died in her stead. This Vivian Mason assumed the identity of Grace Kensington and is now here in Bennett Cove, married to your—" Zeke coughed. "—father."

"So who is Grace Kensington?" I asked.

"Grace Kensington was a woman whose single motivation in life was to find her daughter. They were separated in a horrific train crash in December of 1919. Many people died in the resulting fire. The child was presumed dead, but Mrs. Kensington didn't believe it. She swore her child was alive. It took her months to recover, and since she had no family, there was no one to inquire about the child's welfare while Mrs. Kensington was in the hospital recovering from her injuries. After she got out of the hospital, she set out to find her daughter. It was pure bad luck that she crossed paths with Vivian Mason."

"That is a sad tale," I said. "Did Mrs. Kensington find her daughter?"

"She found her, but she never met her, at least while she was alive." Zeke stared at me, as if calculating just how much he should tell me.

I was tired of secrets. "What? Please tell me."

"I believe you're Grace's daughter."

"That's absurd. I'm Jack and Jessica Bennett's daughter. What a cruel thing to say." I stood up and headed back to Bennett House. I sensed Zeke coming up behind me and broke into a run, but I wasn't fast enough. He grabbed my arm, stopping me before I could get away from him.

"Why would I say that if it wasn't true? She came here looking for you, Sarah. She died. Your stepmother killed her." He thrust the picture of Grace in front of me. "Just look at her. She looks exactly like you."

"That's nonsense. It's not that I don't trust you, Zeke, I do. And I am even willing to believe that my stepmother is a murderer, but adopted? Me? I don't think so."

"Sarah—"

"If I was adopted, I would know. They would have told me."

I had taken the picture of Grace Kensington from

Zeke. I studied it. He was right, there was a resemblance, but lots of unrelated people resembled each other.

"Let's not worry about that right now. I shouldn't have said anything. I'm sorry. Please, don't be angry at me."

"Truce. But you have to admit, it's pretty farfetched." Even as I uttered the words, the probability of the situation sank in. Zeke had nothing but supposition and a photo. He had no proof. "Could Vivian Mason have murdered Gran?"

"I don't know. She didn't have a motive to kill your grandmother. Why would she risk that? If Vivian Mason is a professional, which I believe she is, she would kill to save herself, no question about it. Your Gran may have caught her doing something illegal. Who knows?"

"You think Gran found out who she was, discovered something about her?"

"She could have. It's no secret that your grandmother was more than a little inquisitive," Zeke said.

"She was Bennett Cove's busybody in residence."

"You need to be very careful around Vivian Mason. She's cunning and smart, and she must never know that we are onto her. I've put you in danger by telling you all this. She killed Grace Kensington, and she will kill you if you get in her way."

"If I ask you a question, will you answer me honestly?"

"If I can."

I reminded him of the darkly clad figure I had followed up the mountain trail.

"It was probably Vivian meeting a contact. Did you happen to see a license plate on the car?"

"Couldn't see it. Too dark."

Zeke took a deep breath. He stared out at the ocean for a minute. "Let's get back to the house," he said. "I need to make some phone calls. As for Vivian Mason, I'll see that you're not left alone with her. If things get difficult, we'll move you to a safe location."

"What is the building on the beach? I know it's top secret, but what is it?"

"I'm not entirely certain but if I had to guess, I would say it's an early warning radar station."

"A what?"

"It's a way to track submarines and ships that venture near the coastline. The farmhouse is probably the power station. The barn is probably the ops building, but that is a secret, my love. You best keep clear of the area. You're liable to get shot."

We walked back to the house, arm in arm, until we reached the redwood grove. Under the canopy of the ancient trees, Zeke kissed me once again, before we walked back to the house, careful to keep a respectable distance between us. I wasn't ready for anyone to know that I had fallen in love with Zeke. That was my secret. At least for now.

# CHAPTER 10

Zeke's suggestion that I had been adopted added more stress to an already intolerable situation. So I sought release in physical labor and succeeded in avoiding Zeke, my father, Grace, and everyone else for the rest of the day, as I worked on the most secluded side of the house, away from the road, the front door, and interruption. I channeled the anguish of Gran's murder and Zeke's earlier revelations into physical energy. The autumn chill hung heavy. Soon it would slip away, and winter would be upon us. After Zeke had taken the bulky wrap off my hand, I covered it with a sterile bandage, and slipped my well-worn work gloves over that. Still wearing my heavy sweater, I spent the entire afternoon raking leaves and dead-heading my rose bushes. In the end, I had gone after them with too much zeal and trimmed them down to stubs.

I worked in the garden for several hours, finishing as much of the work as I could without a ladder or a heavy saw. The gutters needed to be cleaned as well, another chore for my to-do list, but not one to be undertaken to-day.

After I finished pruning, I got a can of white paint, added enough paint thinner to get the proper consistency, and spent another hour patching the peeling spots on the front of the house that were within my reach. The newest paint always looked a little different, but sea air was hard on wooden buildings. Patching the rough spots as they appeared was better than having to paint the whole house every five or six years. The sun dipped down over the horizon just as I finished, but I wasn't ready to go in-doors. Strapping on the leather tool belt from the shed, I headed to the front of the house to fix the shutter that hung on hinges so rusted, they turned into orange powder when I tried to remove them. It didn't take me long to replace them with spares and re-hang the shutter. I had the whole job completed in a matter of minutes.

My twelve months at The Laurels had done little for my physical conditioning, so by the time the afternoon slipped into evening, the muscles in my arms and shoul-ders ached. I was tired in the pleasurable way that came from hard, physical labor. I stowed all my tools and headed indoors, longing for a bath and a good meal.

I trudged up to the back porch, lost in my own thoughts, when a flash went off in my face, dazzling and disorienting me. A strange man with a camera and another with a notebook open, pencil at the ready, hurried up to me.

"Miss Bennett, are you a suspect in your grandmother's murder?"

I tried to move to the right, but the man with the notebook moved in cadence with me. I turned around. The man with the camera now stood behind me. They blocked my way into Bennett House. They wouldn't leave me alone until they had what they came for, a story for the front page of the newspaper.

"Miss Bennett," the man with the camera said, "is it true that you've just left an institution for the feeble minded?"

Another flash went off. I put my arm up to shield my eyes.

The back door opened so hard that it slammed against the wall. Zeke burst through it. He came to a stop on the back step, his fists clenched at sides. When he saw the men around me, he seemed to fly toward us. In one fluid movement, he grabbed the camera and flipped it open, exposing the film.

"What do you think you're doing?" The man moved toward Zeke. He threw a punch, but Zeke blocked it. The man reached for his camera, but Zeke, who was taller and quicker, held it just out of reach.

"You're lucky I didn't break it." Zeke handed the camera back to him. "Beat it."

The other man tried to shove his notebook in his pocket, but he fumbled when Zeke approached him and he dropped it. He put his fists up, as if to fight, but when he faced Zeke and had an opportunity to size him up, he ran, leaving the notebook behind.

"I'll track both of you down and beat you senseless if any word about this woman shows up in your papers. Do you understand?" Zeke stood inches away from the camera man's face.

"I'm sorry," the man with the camera said. "I didn't mean no harm." He headed off after his friend.

Zeke put his arm around my shoulders and led me into the house. He shut and locked the door behind me and drew the blinds in the kitchen. "Reporters have been calling all day." He got me a glass of water and handed it to me. "Your father has called Hamish, although I don't see what a lawyer can do about this mess."

"We went through this before, when my mother— when Jessica—fell down the stairs," I said.

"Freedom of the press is great for democracy, but it's problematic when you are the subject of their stories." Zeke stood near the window, peering through the blinds. "I was just about to come out and find you. I'm sorry you had to go through that."

"Hamish will fix it. He did last time, and it was much worse. I don't care what they write about me," I said.

Zeke came over to me. I didn't resist when he wrapped his arms around me.

ᴄ⁄ᴐᴄ⁄ᴐ

Anca, God bless her, had lit a fire in my room. The flickering flames cast their shadows against the wall, making my room warm and inviting. She had started a bath for me and added some soaking salts. Tomorrow I would pay for today's physical exertion, but the bath would help.

I had just taken off my dirty clothes, when she came in carrying a tray bearing fresh-sliced bread with home-made jam and a pot of tea. "You need a snack. You're skin and bones. Eat something. Dinner will be at 8:00 to-night. Miss Grace says you are expected for drinks at 7:30." She placed the tray on my dresser and followed me into the bathroom, where she placed the steaming mug of tea on the side of the tub. "What's happened? You seem different." She scrutinized me.

"I had some interesting news today, Anca, but I promised not to tell anyone. I'm sorry."

She sniffed. I had never kept anything from her be-fore, and hated to do so now.

"Never mind, you are stronger. That is good."

If only it were that simple.

ᴄ⁄ᴐᴄ⁄ᴐ

I awoke the next morning to the sound of rain pelting against my windows. Yet another storm had blown in during the night, giving credence to the weather reports in the newspaper. We were indeed having a rainy October. My muscles ached as I got out of bed, a painful protest to yesterday's physical exertion. I opened my curtains and gazed at the rain. When Anca came into the room, she found me staring out my window.

Together we made my bed, like we had done a thousand times before. I took a sheet out of the basket of clean linens and put it on top of my mattress. In perfect cadence, we tucked in the sheets and blankets, pulled the bedspread up, and fluffed up the pillows.

"Thanks," I said.

"Miss Grace is having breakfast downstairs. I told her to save you some pancakes, but you'll be eating by yourself this morning."

"Where's my father?"

"He is meeting with Mr. Hamish in his office and asked that we not disturb him," Anca said. "Your father made a statement to the reporters. He is famous. They will do what he says."

"Anca, I can help you with chores today. I just have to do something this morning."

"No, dear, but thank you. You are kind to offer." She gave me a wistful smile and slipped out of my room.

I dressed without care in warm pants and a sweater, grabbed my father's rain coat from the hook in the mud room, and headed out the front door, ignoring the rumble in my stomach.

The cold rain had not let up during the short walk to Gran's cottage. Once under the shelter of Gran's porch, I took my raincoat off, shook the water out, and left it on the wicker chair to dry. I kicked off my muddy boots and tucked them under the chair where my coat lay.

In my stocking feet, I let myself in the front door with the key that Gran kept hidden under a pot of ivy. I put the key in my trouser pocket and entered Gran's house, despite Sheriff Carpenter's admonishment.

The house smelled dank and musty, even though it had only been shut up for a short while. I flipped the light switch in the entryway. Nothing.

Gran's electricity was as reliable as that of Bennett House—the first sign of inclement weather and out it went. I got the matches out of the desk and lit one of the many oil lamps that she kept handy.

Someone—in all likelihood Sheriff Carpenter or his young deputy—had been here before me. The papers on top of Gran's desk were no longer in the organized piles that reflected her fastidiousness. They had been rifled through and put back without care.

The drawers had been searched and not closed all the way. Most of Gran's books had been removed from the bookcase.

Some had been tossed back on the shelves, some had been left on the floor.

I went up the stairs to Gran's bedroom. Her essence was so strong here that I needed to pause in the doorway for a moment before I could step inside. It was a timeless room, with a tiny bed set in a wooden bedstead. The floors were wide-planked heart pine, covered with a hundred years' worth of wax. The walls were washed white. Lace curtains hung in the windows. The white cotton sheets and pink counterpane lay in disarray on top of the bed. Someone had rumpled them while searching between the mattresses, which were now crooked. What had they been looking for?

The door to the wardrobe stood open, with all Gran's clothes pushed to one side. Some of them had fallen off their hangers and some lay in a disheveled pile at the bottom. Others had been tossed on the floor in front of the wardrobe, only to be trampled on by uncaring feet. An empty hat box sat on the bed, its lid on the floor. Next to it, the tin box that Gran had used to store my mother's memorabilia had been upended, its contents scattered in a hapless pile and left on the floor. When I saw the pictures, old report cards, a box of baby teeth, a lock of my mother's hair tied with a pink ribbon, my tears flowed unchecked. The realization that Gran was gone for good sank in and settled in my chest like a painful knot.

So I went to work. I hung up Gran's clothes, picked up the scattered contents which surrounded Gran's bed, and didn't stop working until everything in her room was back in place.

THE SPIRIT OF GRACE

Back downstairs, I opened the living room curtains, but the overcast day did little to brighten the interior of the house.

I walked over to Gran's desk, and was just about to sit down, when I noticed the tip of a white envelope sticking out from under the tiny rug upon which the desk sat. Just the tiniest tip of the envelope protruded. I pulled it out and set it on the desk, figuring that it had been kicked under the rug by the police when they tore the place apart during the frenzy after the discovery of Gran's body. The envelope, addressed to my grandmother in very formal handwriting, had a return address in Maine. The envelope's seal had been broken, so I knew Gran had read the letter.

*2 March 1942*

*Dear Madame,*

*My name is Grace Kensington, and although you do not know me, I am anxious to solicit your help. I have written to Mr. Bennett twice, but have yet to receive a response from him. The death of his wife, Jessica, has recently come to light. I am sorry for Mr. Bennett's loss, and for yours; however, my situation is pressing and now I am looking to you for a solution.*

*In December of 1919 my daughter and I were in a terrible train crash while en route to Maine from Canada. I nearly lost my life, and given that many* perished in the accident, it was assumed that the babe in arms with whom I traveled was an unfortunate victim on that sad day. It took me the better part of two years to recover physically from the injuries I sustained in that crash, and although everyone involved in the accident told me otherwise, I always knew deep in my heart that my daughter was alive.

I have spent countless hours tracking down my daughter, Sarah. I have no idea how my injured child came to be adopted by your family, but that does not matter. I am grateful for the love and kindness I am sure you have bestowed upon her.

Now that Sarah Jane is an adult, and in all likelihood forging her own way in this troubled world, I would like to meet her. Do you think she would be amenable to that? I am en route to San Francisco to stay with an aunt as I write this letter. I have enclosed a picture of myself, the newspaper article discussing the accident (to confirm my story, should you have doubts), along with my aunt's address.

I will proceed as you see best, but am quite desperate to meet my daughter, even if it's only from a distance. I must lay eyes upon her. It is that desire which drives me to make this journey.

With Sincere Thanks,
Grace Kensington

ﻭﺳﻭ

My spine tingled as I stared at the two pictures which were enclosed with the letter. One was the same photograph that Zeke had, a portrait of Grace Kensington. The other picture depicted Grace holding a child—me—when I was just a babe. I had a chubby face and rosy cheeks. Grace held me in her arms as my head rested on her shoulder. The sun was in our eyes and we squinted toward the camera, encircled in an aura of happiness.

I dropped the letter on the desk and ran into the bathroom. Had I eaten breakfast, I would have vomited. I bent over the porcelain bowl, heaving and coughing to no avail. When the spasms of nausea subsided, I rinsed my mouth and washed my hands and face with cold water. I stood in front of the small mirror, trying to catch my breath, but unable to do so. I now had absolute proof that my entire life had been a lie. The treachery of it washed over me, the no-nonsense, black-and-white, irrefutable story of my past, and the tragedy that had led me to this place lay before me on the desk of my murdered grandmother.

I went back to the desk, picked up the letter and read it again, and again, and finally, after the third time, the implications contained in it sank in. The death of Grace Kensington, and the reunion we would never have, formed a yawing chasm in the center of my being, resulting in a deep, physical ache. We had just missed knowing each other. How much easier it would have been to accept the story of adoption, if my real mother were there to

explain it to me. As for Grace Kensington, there lay another tragedy, thanks to Vivian Mason.

I don't know how long I sat at Gran's desk, staring at
my mother's picture, the only sound the ticking clock
which had rested on Gran's mantle for decades and the
gentle rain which tapped against the leaded windows.

"Please come to me." I spoke out loud to the empti-
ness, desperate for Grace to appear, as she had so many
times before. "Tell me about the night you died. Tell me
about your murder. Tell me about—" I paused for a second. "Tell me about me."

Silence. I didn't see Grace. I received no sign that
she was with me. But like a jolt of lightening, I was given
the gift of knowledge. The puzzle fit together and understanding flowed through my veins like water in an ever
running stream.

Gran had read this letter before she died. She knew
that the woman my father married was not the real Grace
Kensington. I remembered the night Gran came to the
house, so anxious to speak to my father, so upset that she
gulped Scotch as though it were orange juice. My hands
shook as I tucked the white envelope in the pocket of the
blouse. If Gran confronted Vivian Mason with the
knowledge of her true identity—which Gran was certain
to do—what would Vivian do? According to Zeke, she
would commit murder.

# CHAPTER 11

I put Gran's key back underneath the potted ivy, donned my raincoat and boots, and headed back to Bennett House, not caring if I got wet along the way. Soon I would be cleared of suspicion of Gran's murder. I would point the police to the only person who had a motive to kill Gran.

"Vivian has a motive. Vivian has a motive. Vivian has a motive." I whispered the words out loud in rhythm with my feet as I walked through the rain toward Bennett House.

I barged through the back door, shedding my boots and my coat, leaving them in a pile by the servant's staircase. I hurried through the kitchen, anxious to get upstairs to the privacy of my own room.

"Are you even aware that we are in the room, Sarah

Jane?" my stepmother, Vivian Mason, also known as Grace Kensington, asked.

"I'm sorry. I'm just distracted—"

My father and Vivian had just sat down to lunch at the refectory table in the kitchen. Vivian was doing the serving herself. The smell of chicken noodle soup, a perennial favorite of mine, nauseated me now.

Vivian smiled. My father didn't. He looked at me with concern, but he didn't say a word. *Why didn't you tell me I was adopted?* I wanted to shout. But I didn't say anything out loud, didn't make a scene. Not yet. Vivian Mason, the woman who had murdered the real Grace Kensington, took the napkin from her lap and set it on the table before her. She started to stand up.

"You're soaking wet. Go upstairs and dry off. I'll bring you some soup."

"No, I don't want anything from you."

"Sarah Jane?" Concern echoed in my father's voice.

"Thank you, but I'm not hungry." I smiled, forcing my words to sound receptive to my stepmother's feigned kindness. "I'm just here to change clothes before I go into town."

"I'll drive you." Vivian looked at me through knowing eyes, as if she was privy to everything I knew, as if she had planned this whole scenario, and I was just a puppet, a player in some macabre game.

"I'd prefer to just go alone, if you don't mind. You don't mind if I use the car, do you?"

"Of course not," my father said.

I hurried out of the room before they could speak to me further, before Vivian could finagle a ride into town or otherwise get the car away from me.

I stopped for a second in the foyer, looking at the portraits of my grandfather, my great grandfather, and their respective wives. These men were no relation to me. I had no attachment to them or to Bennett House. Jack Bennett had always been kind to me, and even though he wasn't my real father, we would always have a relationship, no matter where I lived. But nothing held me here. Nothing tied me to this place. I could pack a bag and leave this afternoon if I wanted to. But I didn't want to, not until Vivian Mason was punished for murdering my mother and Gran.

Zeke's voice cut through my thoughts. He spoke from the phone in the office with the door open, his voice louder than usual. He wasn't scheduling an appearance for my father this time. He spoke German, and although I couldn't understand the meaning of his words, their tone conveyed anguish. The door to the office was open. Zeke stood with his back toward me. His shoulders, so strong and broad, were hunched, as though unable to handle the burden being placed on them. I listened to him speak, heard the catch in his voice as he fought back tears. When he hung up the phone and turned around to me, his face was pale. The tears filled his eyes, making the green of them shimmer like emeralds. Zeke tried to blink them away, but they spilled down his cheeks. My heart broke for him, for us, for the unknown tragedy that he held inside.

I opened my arms to him. He stood up and stepped into them as though it was the most natural thing to do. I led him over to the sofa, where we sat down, never breaking our physical connection. I held him like a baby as he cried violent, wracking sobs that shook his body and took his breath away.

I didn't let go. I held him to my breast, murmuring the assuring words that I had often wished someone would say to me when I was alone and afraid and in need of comfort. "It's all right. You'll be okay. I'm here. It's all right." I murmured the same phrases over and over again, until the sobbing was reduced to a ragged breathing and stopped completely.

Whatever Zeke was going through, whatever he had done, I would face it with him.

He pulled away from me, took a handkerchief out of his trouser pocket, and blew his nose. He didn't say anything about the intimate moment we had just shared. He didn't speak at all. He just stared at me with those green eyes, now rimmed with red. After he put his handkerchief away, he took my hand and kissed my fingers. He tucked a stray lock of hair behind my ear. When he took his hand away, the heat from his touch lingered on my skin, a burning reminder of my desire for him.

"Do you want to talk?" I asked.

"My older brother, William, was picked up by the Gestapo."

"Oh, I'm so sorry. There has to be something we can do," I said, in a feeble attempt to provide him some glimmer of hope.

"There's nothing anyone can do. They come for you, they take you, torture you, and, if you're lucky, they kill you. I was with him. We went over together in the summer of 1939. My father charged William and me with the responsibility of getting my aunts and cousins back to America. William was to stay and deal with some financial issues. My father hoped to smuggle my aunts' fortune out, too. I should have been the one to stay, not William." He stood up and walked over to the window, where he stood with his back to me. "I feel guilty for being alive."

I stood and went to him. I grabbed his hand in mine. "Please don't say that."

"Sarah, don't," he said, brushing my hand away.

He turned around, came back to the couch, sat down next to me, and took my hand. "We need to talk. I'm sorry if I gave you the wrong impression. I know we shared some intimate moments these past few days, and I shouldn't have led you on like that."

"I don't understand."

"I have things in my life that need to be sorted out before I fall in love—get involved."

"So what happened between us—" I couldn't say it

out loud, couldn't ask if the kisses we shared were real. It was too late for me.

Zeke didn't say anything. He let go of my hand.

"I'm not saying never; I'm just saying not now. I need time. I'm sorry, Sarah. I hope you can forgive me." He didn't meet my eyes as he stood up and walked out of the room.

I loved Zeke. I wanted him with a passion, the likes of which I had never known before. He needed time. I would give him that. There would be no more stolen kisses, no arms wrapped around me, no one to lean on during this time of revelation and change. I was alone— as I had always been. I bit back tears as I headed up the stairs to my room.

The letter I had stolen from Gran's desk was now tucked away in the breast pocket of my blouse. I didn't remember putting it there. The urgency of my new-found information, Vivian Mason's motive for Gran's murder, paled in comparison to Zeke's news.

I would call Sheriff Carpenter and tell him what I had found. I would turn the letter from Grace Kensington to Gran over to him and let him deal with Vivian Mason. But the phone lines at Bennett House—and in Bennett Cove for that matter—were not secure, and I knew without question that my conversation with Sheriff Carpenter should be private.

If I discussed my stepmother's true identity with the sheriff over the phone, the news would be all over town by tomorrow morning. No, I would have to speak with Sheriff Carpenter in person.

Up in my room, I changed into a sensible gray wool skirt and a pale blue cardigan, along with my mother's pearls. I combed my hair, pinned it up, and drove into town in the rain, only to discover that Sheriff Carpenter was in San Rafael for the day and wouldn't return to his office until tomorrow afternoon.

By the time I got back home, my stomach growled from hunger. I needed to eat but couldn't bear to face my father and Vivian. Luckily for me, they would be going out tonight. My father was going to read excerpts from his book at a party in San Rafael. Zeke would serve as chauffeur, in case too many martinis were consumed. I would be home alone this evening. Anca brought up a tray of bread and butter and a mug of hot tea. After she left, I stayed in my room with the door locked, so as to not be interrupted. I tried to read my father's book, but I couldn't focus and read the same sentence over and over.

As if driven by an unforeseen force, I took the letter out of my pocket and read it. My reading alternated with trips to the window, where I would watch the rain as it formed a pool in the low part of the gravel drive. Then, because I had no self-control to do otherwise, I would open the letter and read it again, and yet again. I read until my eyes burned and the words were seared into my memory.

I was awakened by my father, Vivian, and Zeke leaving in the car. The rain had stopped, leaving the air brisk and clean in its wake. I had spent hours in my room and was antsy from being cooped up. I didn't light any candles. Instead, I fumbled in the dark for warm outdoor clothing, and bundled up in a warm navy pea coat and a wool stocking cap. Armed with a thermos of hot tea to stave off the chill, a cheese sandwich for my dinner, and a canvas cushion to sit on, I set out into the night toward the beach for a solitary picnic.

ᘓᘏᘓ

I stayed in the dunes until I found a secluded spot. As I set down my cushion and laid out my unglamorous dinner fare, I considered what a good spy I would make. I knew the hills and trails around Bennett Cove better than any of those soldiers. I could sneak a cannon in from San Francisco if I put my mind to it.

The cushion on the sand kept me dry. I was content in the night air, eating my sandwich and drinking hot tea, while the waves pounded the shore and the stars pulsed in the October sky. When I finished eating, I leaned back on my elbows, content, undisturbed until the cold sea air, which had been seeping through the legs of my trousers, became unbearable.

I packed up my dinner leavings, put the top on the thermos, picked up the cushion, and was ready to head back home when I saw the flashing lights. They weren't random or arbitrary. They were a signal—two short blips before a long flash. The same pattern repeated two or three times and stopped. The signals came from the mountain behind me. I guessed they originated from one of the empty cabins that were let to summer tourists prior to the war. The cabins were rustic affairs, with wooden shutters for windows and no running water. The campers would bring their own cots, beds, cooking stoves, and other supplies. The tourists didn't mind the lack of modern accoutrements, as the breathtaking views of the Pacific Ocean in all her glory made any inconvenience well worth the trouble.

I stood up and craned my neck, trying to pinpoint the exact location of the lights, but they had stopped. Across town, from a point down by the water, on the opposite edge of the beach, another set of lights answered. My pulse quickened. After the light by the water blinked a few times, the light on the mountainside blinked its response.

Carrying my thermos and cushion, I ran toward home, kicking the sand up behind me, cringing as it seeped into my shoes, underneath my socks. I burst through the front door, through the foyer, through the library, and into my father's office. I gasped for breath. Rivulets of sweat ran down my face and between my shoulder blades.

Anca had stoked the fire, even though no one would be using the office until my father and Vivian returned from their evening out. The room was aglow with its licking flames. Newspaper and magazines cluttered the desks, and piles of fan mail sat on Zeke's desk, to be dealt with tomorrow.

I picked up the phone, and after what seemed an eternity was connected to Colonel Matthews.

I told him what I had seen, the lights, clearly a coded signal, and the response.

"Thank, you, my dear. We are aware of it."

"Were you able to discover who was up there?"

"I will tell you that arrests have been made, but I cannot discuss more than that."

Any enthusiasm I had for pursing the matter further waned when the exhaustion from this long day washed over me. I hauled myself up to bed, ready for it to be over.

# CHAPTER 12

I had disturbing nightmares and awoke shivering, the covers in a pile on the floor. I dreamt of violent fighting, of the peaceful beaches of Bennett Cove being invaded by Japanese and Germans alike. The soldiers knew where we lived and where we kept our valuables. They looted our banks, ransacked our homes, kidnapped our children, and destroyed our democracy, all enabled by Vivian Mason, the spy in our midst. Vivian couldn't be captured. She outwitted everyone who went after her. I dreamt Hitler drove his tanks right up to our front door and was about to burst through it and into our foyer when I awoke, more exhausted than if I hadn't slept at all.

I lit the candle next to my bed and took it with me as

I headed down to the kitchen for a mug of cocoa. I reckoned that I would read my father's book until I fell back asleep and remembered that I had left it downstairs earlier. I was one of those readers that read every book written by an author that I liked. I could read the same Margery Allingham novel over and over, and find something new and delightful every time.

Once downstairs, I headed into the library. The dwindling fire and the light from my candle provided all the light I needed. I had fetched my book and was about to head into the kitchen to make cocoa when the sound of drawers opening and shutting and papers rustling came from my father's office. Newspaper reporters again? Would they be so bold as to break into the house? Of course, they would. I ducked into a cranny next to an unwieldy piece of furniture that was as old as Bennett House and tried to still my heart while someone searched through my father's office.

I grabbed the shotgun by the front door, cocked it, and walked back to the office, careful not to step on the boards that I knew would creak. I stepped into the room, pointing the gun at Vivian Mason, who was now seated at my father's big wooden desk. An oil lamp was lit and cast a faint glow over the things she had laid out on the blotter. I moved closer to her and recognized my passport, my birth certificate, the paperwork concerning the inheritance from my mother, along with the deeds to Bennett House and other property my father owned. She was dressed in a warm navy coat and wore a black watchman's cap. A pair of black leather gloves lay on the desk near her. She looked up at me, saw the shotgun I held trained on her, and gasped.

"What in the world are you doing with that thing?"

"What are you doing with my personal papers?" I asked.

Vivian placed her hands on the desk. "Sarah, please put the gun down. Everything will be all right."

"Quit talking to me like I'm crazy." I engaged the safety before I leaned the gun against the wall. "It's 2:00 a.m. What are you doing up at this hour, going through my papers?" I moved toward the woman who had taken my mother's name, who in all likelihood murdered her in cold blood.

When I got close to the desk, she wiped her forearm across it, sweeping the papers back into the strong box, closed the lid, and put the box back into the drawer from which she had taken it.

"I could ask you the same thing. I have as much right to be here as you do."

"I couldn't sleep." I held up my book. "Getting a book from the library isn't the same as snooping through my father's desk."

"You've found out, haven't you? That you're adopted..." Her voice trailed off as she looked at me expectantly.

She bent her head, as if she were in prayer. Her dark

hair fell away from the back of her neck, revealing the
alabaster skin and the subtle outline of the vertebrae
there. She raised her head and took a deep breath before
she spoke. "I need to speak to you, Sarah. I've been keeping the truth from you and Jack. Now that you grandmother's been—I'm sorry. This is so awful."

She massaged her forehead with her fingers and
sighed. I had to give credit where due. This woman was a
master. If I hadn't known that my stepmother was a ruthless murderer, I would have believed her without question.

"I'm not really Grace Kensington. I have lied to everyone and now I'm headed for big trouble." She shivered
and rubbed her arms. "God, it's freezing in here."

I wanted to jump over the desk, pick her up by the
scruff of her neck, and shake her until she confessed to
Grace Kensington's—my real mother's—murder. By the
grace of God, I didn't.

"Before I came here, I was married to a man who
drank to excess and beat me for sport. He spent most of
his time at the bars—thank goodness—but he would get
liquored up and come home to me. When we were first
married, his abuse was limited to an occasional slap
across the face. As time went on, the slap across the face
became an open handed hit to the jaw, which became a
push to the floor, then kicks while I was down. The pro-
gression was self-evident.

Before I left, the beatings had become so severe I

knew it was only a matter of time before he would kill me. So I decided to leave. I secured a job in a different town and fled in the night with the clothes on my back. I made a clean getaway and assumed the idiot would wake up the next morning, find me gone, and maybe find some other woman to terrorize.

"I became a companion and caregiver to a dear old soul named Joyce Kensington—your great aunt—in San Francisco. She provided room and board, and a small salary. She was kind and easy to work for. We got along well, and I was fond of her. It wasn't too long after I started working for her that her great-niece, Grace Kensington, came to visit from Maine. Turns out Grace had a long-lost daughter whom she had tracked down to San Francisco."

The blood pounded in my ears. I grabbed the back of the chair by Zeke's desk for support.

"For a while, everything was fine. I let myself believe I had gotten away from Tom for good. Life went on, it was boring, but I was safe and somewhat content. One day as I was changing the sheets for Miss Joyce, I happened to look out the window. There, at the edge of her property, stood Tom. I could tell by the look on his face that he meant to kill me. I didn't know what to do. If I called the police, they would in all likelihood send me home with my abusive husband. I decided to at least tell Miss Joyce about him. I owed her that much. I would collect my things, leave, and let things unfold as they would.

But when I went inside, Joyce asked me to go to the store on an errand. And I formulated a plan.

"I managed to pull the car out of the garage and drive to the store, where I used a public phone to call the police and report a burglar at Joyce's house. I waited long enough for the police to arrive and escort Tom off the property, but when I arrived back at Joyce's, the house was in flames. Your mother and her aunt—your great aunt—were in it." She rubbed her eyes, as if to block out the imagery. "It was awful. I couldn't get to them. I swear, I tried, but the heat of the fire, the smoke, it was impossible to save them.

"The fire department came. There were police cars everywhere. I told the authorities that I was Grace Kensington. I knew enough about your mother's past to lie, and no one found out. My passport was replaced, and I came here. I figured this was where your mother was headed, that maybe I owed it to her to see you, to make sure you were okay. It was pure coincidence that your father—Jack Bennett—and I met and fell in love."

"But my mother is older than you. Didn't anyone question the age difference? You don't look anything like her. Surely they would check the picture." My voice held the appropriate shock and mortification that it should have held, had I believed Grace's story and been surprised at it, but I didn't believe her. Not one word. Not for one minute.

"Apparently not, or I wouldn't be sitting here."

I couldn't believe she could make up such a scenario, and I was once again surprised at her cleverness. "So what are you going to do?" I asked.

"I'm going to tell Jack tomorrow. I owe him the truth. After that, I will speak to Sheriff Carpenter. But I wanted to tell you first. It seemed the decent thing to do. There's something else, Sarah."

I waited for her to continue.

"I've seen the way you look at Zeke, seen the stolen kisses."

"I—"

"Don't bother trying to deny it. It's obvious you are in love with him, and he's in love with you, but he probably gave you some story about how he's not available because his soul is tortured. Ah, I can see, by the look in your eyes, that's exactly what happened. Have you ever wondered what he's doing here? It's quite evident he has no aptitude for copy editing or research. He makes appointments and keeps Jack's calendar, but anyone could do that, even you. Jack tolerates him because he has a kind heart. Did you know Zeke speaks German? Have you considered that he's the spy? He may have murdered your grandmother. I just don't want you blindsided. I know you don't like me, but I am offering you this advice."

"Thanks for your concern, but there's nothing between Zeke and me. I don't wish to discuss it further."

"Okay," Vivian said. "I just don't want you to get

hurt. Oh, I can see I've made you angry. I'm sorry. I thought you'd resigned yourself to being a spinster."

"Tell my father who you are, or I will," I said, unable to resist the urge to get the last word in.

I retrieved the shotgun I had leaned against the wall. Rather than putting it back by the front door, I took it to my room with me. '*I thought you'd resigned yourself to being a spinster.*' Vivian's words rang in my ears as I climbed the stairs. Once in my room, I locked my door and put the shot gun on the floor under my bed. I tried to sleep, but Vivian's story, her accusations against Zeke made my blood boil.

Spinster indeed.

# CHAPTER 13

I awoke the next morning to the sounds of Anca and Vivian Mason screaming at each other downstairs. Quiet, sweet tempered Anca shouted at Vivian in her native tongue. Vivian yelled back, her voice shrill and becoming louder by the minute.

The clock next to my bed said 10:00 a.m. My head ached. I threw on clothes and headed down stairs, not caring what my hair looked like or that I hadn't even washed my face. With any luck, I could break up their fight before it got out of hand.

They faced each other in the foyer. Anca had her arms crossed over her bosom, her hip thrust out to the side, and a determined look on her face that I found somewhat frightening as I had never seen it before. The

basket of linens sat on the floor by her feet. My stepmother wore a navy dress, complete with matching shoes.
On the foyer table lay a hat, her handbag, and the white
gloves she would need if she were going to the city. Her
arms were rigid at her sides, her hands clenched in tight
fists. Neither one of them noticed me as I walked down
the stairs.

"You work for this family, you work for me. I've
asked you twenty times to dust the bookcases in Jack's
office. Twenty times. They are filthy. I have asked you to
sweep the floor in the larder. You have not done it."

"I have been cleaning this house for twenty years."
Anca spoke English now. "I don't need you to tell me
how to do my job."

I stood at the bottom of the staircase, waiting for an
opening, an opportunity to jump into the fray.

"I've asked you to rearrange the bowls and cutlery in
the kitchen, but you haven't done it. I've asked you to
straighten my closet. You haven't done it." My stepmother looked at me out of the corner of her eye. "I've had it
with you, Anca. You clearly have been spoiled and have
forgotten your place in this family. I'm not going to stand
here and argue with a servant."

"I too have had enough. I quit. I'll leave tomorrow
morning."

"No," I said, "Anca, please—"

"Sarah, you're part of the problem. You treat her like
she's family. She's a servant, for heaven's sakes."

"She is part of the family, and she's not quitting." I walked over to Anca and placed a hand on her shoulder. "Are you, dear? You're not going to leave us because of a simple misunderstanding, are you?"

"It's no use." Anca shook her head. "She is not a great lady, like Sarah, like her mother, Jessica. This house is not the same and I will no longer stay here." She looked at me with sad eyes. "I will take the bus early tomorrow morning." She picked up her basket of dirty linens and walked toward the corridor, her head held high, her pride intact.

"Did you have to pick a fight with her?"

"Don't blame me for this," my stepmother said.

"She takes care of this entire house by herself. It's too much for one person, and it's not your place to fire her."

"I suppose you think that it's your place?"

I considered her question and realized that I was no longer sure. "Stay away from Anca." I turned my back and walked away.

❧❧❧

I found Anca in the back hallway, loading the sheets into the washer. I watched her for a few minutes as she bent over the basket, shook out the sheets, and put them in the washing machine. Anca preferred to do the laundry the old-fashioned way, but she had since come to like the quick efficiency of loading the dirty clothes into "that contraption," adding the detergent, and presto, work finished. On cold days, Anca would string our clean laundry on a clothes line through the kitchen, letting the warmth of the stove dry the clothes, never mind that every now and then the sheets would smell like a pork roast or a loaf of bread.

Now I watched her, sad at the changes wrought by time. When had her hair become so gray? When had her back developed that slight hump between the shoulder blades? Anca was close to seventy years old. I always assumed that she would be with us forever. Where would she go when she could no longer work, when her old bones wouldn't allow her to do anything but rest and read and knit sweaters for her sister's grandchildren? Anca had lost all of her own offspring, every single one of them had died a tragic death, like so many of the Roma had suffered in Europe. Who would tend to Anca when she was too old to work?

She stood up straight and rubbed the small of her back with her work worn hand, the knuckles reddened and chapped.

"I feel your eyes upon me, Sarah," she said. She turned around and smiled. "Don't worry yourself about what happened earlier. I was going to talk to you about quitting anyway."

"Really?"

"I'm tired," she said. "Your mother—Jessica—left

me a little money. If I'm careful, I can live on it for the rest of my life."

"Where will you go?" I asked.

"My sister is lonely, she wants me to come to her," she said. "She has a small bedroom for me. She has everything I need." Anca's sister lived in San Francisco. Her two sons had joined the Navy. One of them was injured during the Battle of the Midway and was recuperating at a hospital in some undisclosed location. The other one was a pilot. Anca was very proud of her nephews.

"So you'll be close, and I can see you often," I said.

Anca put a hand on my cheek. She had tears in her eyes. "You can see me often, Sarah, but it's time for you to move on. You know that, don't you?"

I nodded, knowing full well that after I was able to prove what Vivian Mason did, what she had done to my real mother, Grace Kensington, I would leave Bennett Cove. Anca was right. It was time for me to move on.

ℰↃℰↃ

I dressed and combed my hair before I went into the office to write Anca her final check. I glanced at Zeke's desk as I walked by. He had prepared a checklist of the tasks he needed to do this morning to finalize my father's trip to New York. The list included things like confirming my father's reservation at the Algonquin, scheduling lunch with various important people at 21 and Tavern on the Green, and other mundane tasks. My father was a celebrity now, and Zeke was charged with keeping his calendar in order, typing his correspondence, and dealing with Hamish, who I knew called every day, eager for news about the latest book.

I sat down at my father's desk and pulled out the household account ledger. I wrote Anca's check, a full month's wages, plus six months as severance. As I put the checkbook back in the drawer, I discovered the lid to the strongbox wasn't all the way shut. I tried to push the lid down, but the lock wouldn't catch. I took the box out of the drawer and set it on top of my father's desk. The papers that Vivian had taken out last night were out of sorts and thrown back into the box in a disorganized pile that prevented the lid from closing.

I dumped everything out and sorted the pile so it was small and compact. There were the property deeds, banking documents, and other items that Vivian had pilfered through last night. The stacked papers felt strange, not the right thickness. Something was missing. I rifled them and discovered my birth certificate and passport were no longer there. I went through the papers again, checking to make sure that I hadn't overlooked them. They were gone. Vivian had taken them.

Acting without a thought to the promise I made to Vivian about giving her twenty-four hours before I spoke to my father, I barged up the stairs. He needed to know the woman he married was not Grace Kensington. He needed to know what his wife had done to Gran. He needed to know that his wife had taken my birth certificate and passport. I flew up the stairs, but stopped just short of bursting into the room. Vivian and Jack were having a somewhat heated conversation. I pressed my ear against the door, and eavesdropped without shame.

"I'm not exactly in funds, darling," Vivian said.

"You misled me about your financial situation," my father said.

Vivian said something to him, but I couldn't make out her words.

"Are you keeping any other secrets from me?" my father asked.

Vivian murmured something in return.

"Of course, I'll help you. You're my wife. I'll give you anything you need."

Somehow this dialogue between them brought home the seriousness of the situation. Zeke's words of caution rang through my ears. I took a deep breath, vowed to be calm and rational, and knocked on the door.

"Come in," my father said. When Vivian saw me, she forced a smile, but underneath it was just the slightest hint of unease. She kissed my father and headed toward the door where I stood.

"Remember your promise," she whispered when she passed me, in a voice just soft enough for my ears only.

"Before you go," I said, loud enough for my father to hear, "did you take my passport and birth certificate while you were looking through the desk last night? They're missing and since you were the last one..." I let my words hang in the air.

"Of course I didn't take your passport. Why in the world would I do that?"

"One wonders," I said.

"Now if you'll excuse me." She shut the door behind her, leaving me alone with my father.

The dark velvet curtains had been pulled over the windows, and the fire and two oil lamps provided the only light in the room. Two club chairs faced the fireplace, with a marble topped table between them. My father sat in one of the chairs, on the other, a notebook sat open, a pencil resting on the page. I was about to pick it up when my father reached over and snatched the notebook away, snapping it shut in one fell swoop.

"No, Sarah, no one gets to read my work until it's finished." His smile took the sting out of his sharp words. "What can I do for you?" He beckoned to the empty chair where the notebook had lain. I sat down in it. "Sarah Jane? What's wrong?"

"I know I'm adopted."

He looked at me with the sad eyes of a man who has lost his wife and is now afraid of losing his daughter. My heart broke for him. "Sit down," he said.

I sat in the empty chair and waited for him to explain.

"How did you find out?"

I wasn't prepared for this question. Admitting the truth would betray Zeke's confidence. So I lied. "I found some notes in Gran's desk. A letter, actually."

"Can I see it?" He asked.

"I burned it." Another lie.

"I'm sorry that you had to find out like that. Your mother—Jessica—insisted that we never tell you. I didn't agree with her. I wanted to tell you—you cannot know how many times I almost told you, I was so desperate not to have secrets from you. When Jessica died, I vowed to tell you the truth. But you went away, and when you came home, I didn't want to upset you, not after the other thing—my getting married." He closed his eyes and took a deep breath. "And here we are."

"Yes, here we are."

"Can you ever forgive me?"

"I already have. You're the only father I've ever known. We've forged a relationship over the years that no one will replace. That will never change."

He smiled at me with sad eyes. "Thank you for that."

"Do you know anything about my birth family?"

"I know your mother was killed in a train crash while en route from Canada to Maine in December of 1919. I know that your father died of influenza in 1918. Most of all, I know Jessica and I loved you the second we saw you."

His face looked ashen. He had circles under his eyes, and for a moment I wondered if he were ill.

"Are you all right?"

"No, I'm not. I am a man who has made a huge mistake."

"Are you talking about—"

"My marriage? Yes. What was I thinking, marrying a woman who is so much younger than I?"

"Perhaps you were flattered?" I wanted to scream out what I knew about Vivian, but didn't dare. At some point I would tell my father exactly what his wife was. Now was not the time.

"I was a fool. Never mind that. I'm sorry I need to cut this conversation short, but I need to finish packing. Zeke is driving me to the airport this afternoon." He stood up and walked over to his bed, where he flipped open the lid of his suitcase.

"Did Viv—Grace tell you that Anca quit?"

He put a stack of folded shirts into his suitcase. "Not only does Grace have a hot temper, she is impetuous, and I'm sorry if she showed Anca disrespect. Surely you didn't expect Anca to live with us and take care of you forever."

"I don't think this was planned," I said. "She never mentioned it to me."

"Sarah, Anca told me that she was planning on leaving. I didn't tell you because she wanted to be the one to do it. This little spat with my wife just hurried the inevitable." He put two pairs of pajamas into the case and shut the lid once again.

"So that's that," I said, resigned to the idea of life without Anca.

"I'm afraid so."

"Do you mind if I use the car to run into town before you leave?" I asked.

"Sure, just be back in an hour."

I kissed his cheek and headed back to my room. I took the letter that I had stolen from Gran's office, and put it in my purse, where I knew it would be safe from prying eyes. If I hurried, I could make it to town, speak to Sheriff Carpenter, and be back before my father had to leave for the airport. The sheriff needed to know that Vivian had a motive. I didn't have to go far. He and Zeke were in my father's office, talking to each other in lowered voices. They stopped talking when I came into the room. Zeke smiled at me briefly, but he wouldn't meet my eyes.

"Oh, I was just coming to see you," I said to Sheriff Carpenter. I wondered if he had ever investigated a murder before, never mind that the victim was someone with whom he had more than a passing acquaintance. The sheriff and Gran were old friends, and I had often wondered if Sheriff Carpenter held a torch for my strong-willed grandmother.

"What can I do for you, Sarah Jane?"

I had Zeke's attention now, too. I shut the office door and walked over to his desk. He had sat down, and Sheriff Carpenter was perched on the corner, one leg swinging. I took the letter my mother had written to Gran and handed it to Sheriff Carpenter.

"When did you find that?" Zeke asked.

"Yesterday. I meant to tell you after I found it but—" I didn't want to remind him of our conversation, the tragedy that befell him, and the honesty which put a chasm between us that now seemed insurmountable.

"Where did you say you found this?" Sheriff Carpenter asked. The hand that held the letter trembled.

"Gran's house," I said. Before Sheriff Carpenter could scold, I rambled on. "I know I wasn't supposed to go in there, but everyone thinks I'm the one who killed her, just because of what happened to my mother."

"What did you hope to find?" At least he had enough tact to refrain from scolding me.

"I don't know. I just searched the house. The envelope was sticking out from underneath the carpet in the living room."

"Well, I would say Vivian Mason has motive to kill Gran." Zeke had read the letter and handed it back to Sheriff Carpenter.

The sheriff put it in his shirt pocket. "Miss Bennett— Sarah, we never thought you were a suspect. We just didn't want Vivian—your stepmother—to know we are watching her."

"I'm certain this woman murdered the real Grace Kensington. What are we going to do about that?" I asked.

"Nothing, right now," the sheriff said.

"My mother's murder—and her aunt's—are just not important, I guess." I couldn't keep the sarcasm from my voice. "My god, she burned them alive! Doesn't anyone care about that? Why is that not important?"

"Think before you shout." Zeke stood up from the desk and leaned close to me. "She'll hear you, and then we'll have bigger problems," he whispered.

"Don't you touch me," I hissed, wriggling out of his grasp.

My words cut Zeke. The hurt flashed through his eyes. He recoiled and stepped away. The muscles along his jaw line flexed as he clenched his teeth. He was angry at me now.

I didn't care. I was tired of being brushed aside and lied to.

"This whole case is going to be turned over to the FBI. They want to find out who this woman is working with and what she actually knows. We've received intelligence that has led to a smattering of arrests over the past few days, but no one's talking—they're afraid of whoever they answer to, the higher-ups in the organization. Once we get a handle on the magnitude of their operation, they will investigate the murders that she committed. Meanwhile, you need to stay out of her way." Sheriff Carpenter spoke in a soft voice that I had to strain to hear. "I wonder if we should move you someplace safe."

"Won't that be a little suspicious? I think I should

stay here and carry on as usual. She doesn't suspect anything."

"I won't let anything happen to her," Zeke said.

"I'm a phone call away. You can call me any time,
even at home. Okay? You have my number?"

"Thanks," I said.

"I'm sorry that you have to go through all this. We'll
get her for your grandmother's murder, and we'll get her
for Grace Kensington's murder too. I promise you that,"
Sheriff Carpenter said as he stood up.

After he had gone, Zeke and I were alone in the office. Zeke fidgeted with the papers on his desk. He
looked at me as if he wanted to say something, but
changed his mind. When he turned his attention back to
his notebooks and lists, I walked out of the room.

# CHAPTER 14

Once in my room, I closed the door and leaned against it for a moment, glad for the sanctuary of my own space. I sat on the bed, not quite sure what to do with myself. Zeke had gotten the car from the garage. From the vantage point of my window, I watched as he pulled the car up to the front door. He turned off the engine. I heard footsteps on the gravel below and my father's voice as he spoke to Zeke. Their voices were clear and easy to hear through my window, which was cracked open for fresh air.

"You've taken care of my reservations at the Algonquin?"

"I reserved a suite. Your luncheon appointments and speaking engagements are confirmed and noted in your calendar. You were going to make your own dinner plans."

"That's right. Good man."

The car doors slammed, Zeke loaded the luggage in the trunk, and soon the car drove away, leaving Anca and me alone with Vivian. I would rest easier when Zeke was back from the airport. After my father was settled in at the Algonquin, I would call him and tell him everything I had discovered about his wife. Telling him was the decent thing to do, and I wasn't going to wait until he got home. I'd call him, never mind the continual admonition over the radio and in the newspapers about using the phone lines for unnecessary long-distance calls. I knew that the telephone lines needed to be kept free for the war effort and should only be used in an emergency. This was an emergency.

ℰↃℰↃ

When the pipes started banging as Vivian drew her bath, I eased out my bedroom door, careful not to make any noise, and tip-toed down the hall to her bedroom. I stood still, and listened until the bathwater stopped running. Copying the detectives in the mysteries that I loved, I used an unbent hairpin as a key, sticking into the keyhole like I had seen in the movies and wriggling it until the lock gave way. I had never ventured into lock picking before, but the locks on the interior doors at Bennett

House were simple enough to make my task easy. I crossed over the threshold and into her room.

After a minute my eyes adjusted to the dark. I could see Vivian had made a lot of changes to this room she had claimed as her own. Midnight blue curtains now hung in the windows. She had painted the room a shade of light blue, which reminded me of the beach in summertime. The bed, a mahogany four-poster that had been taken from the guest room down the hall—God only knows how she managed to move it—was covered with a white counterpane.

She had chosen the most valuable knickknacks from those that were scattered around the house. I recognized a Limoges vase that Gran had given to my adoptive mother, Jessica, along with a silver inkwell that had belonged to my great grandfather. She had taken two silver candelabras from the dining room. They each held five white tapered candles, which now provided sufficient light to make the room stylish and inviting despite the lack of electricity. The seascapes that she stole from my room now hung over the small secretary that she used for a writing desk. I wanted to snatch the pictures off the wall, but thought better of it. Logic and reason needed to guide me now.

I froze as the bathroom door started to open, then I flew into the open wardrobe and tucked myself in the farthest corner. Vivian came into the room, unaware that I hid in her big armoire, not three feet from where she stood, watching every move she made. Through the hanging dresses that served as my camouflage, I saw her bare feet, pale and white with toes painted blood red. She set the lone candle she carried on her dresser, walked over to the wardrobe, and came to a stop inches away from me. I held my breath as she took a peignoir off one of the hangers before closing the wardrobe door and returning to the bathroom.

After several minutes had passed, I stepped out, still and silent until Vivian was back in the tub, humming and splashing. I moved catlike through the room, opening the drawers to her nightstand, her dresser, her desk, looking for my passport and birth certificate and for anything that would tie her to my mother, Grace Kensington, and expose her for what she was. I needed to do this—this was my way of avenging Grace Kensington's death—but my search was in vain. I could have searched the pockets of Vivian's clothes, but it would take too long to rifle through every garment.

An old leather satchel lay open on the bed. I opened it up and fished around inside to find a compact, a wallet, and an old tube of lipstick. I opened the wallet—empty. My birth certificate and passport weren't in this room. Where would I hide something if I didn't want anyone else to find it? I turned around, taking in my surroundings as a whole.

I was about to abandon my search all together, when I noticed that the mattress was crooked on the bed, as though someone had changed the sheets, but hadn't bothered to put things back. I ran my hand between the mattress and the box spring and found an envelope made of thick paper fastened shut with a bendable metal clasp. I pulled it out of its hiding place. Before I opened it, I listened to make sure Vivian was still in the tub. The splashing had stopped and the room was silent. I hoped that she had leaned back and was soaking in the scented bubbles.

I unbent the metal clasps, opened the envelope, and pulled a piece of microfilm, thin as paper yet stiff as cardboard. I held the film up to the light, but couldn't make out the imagery on it. Not sure what to do, I put it back in the envelope and in turn slid the envelope back between the mattress and box spring.

I had read about devices that spies used to convey messages. Ingenious inventions, such as cameras shaped like pens and tubes of lipstick were standard fare for a modern spy. I wasn't surprised that my stepmother would carry microfilm. Here was evidence of her treasonous activities. What to do about it? Nothing. I would wait until Zeke got home.

Back in my own room, I locked the door behind me. I stoked the fire and curled up with my father's book. His storytelling didn't captivate me like the British mysteries that I favored, but there was something about my father's prose that I found familiar and comfortable.

I enjoyed the novel's premise, wherein a young woman attends college, despite the obstacles put before

her due to her sex. Of course, someone is murdered and
the heroine is the suspect. She solves the crime and wins
the affection of her young, handsome professor, with
whom she falls in love. My father's characters had depth
and breadth to them and were crafted with a sensitivity
that was almost feminine. I had no idea my father could
write at all, never mind step out of himself so completely.
He had channeled Jessica's death and the ensuing grief
into something positive, for Jessica's influence was everywhere in the book. Some of the main character's man-
nerisms and colloquialisms I recognized as hers.

When I finished reading, I closed the book and set it
on my nightstand. At least now I could say that I had indeed read my father's debut novel and discuss it with him
if the need arose. I picked up *The Circular Staircase* by
Mary Roberts Rinehart, a perennial favorite that I would
read next, and soon became lost in the story.

The sun was starting to go down when Anca knocked
on my door. My stepmother had requested a dinner tray
in her room, so Anca and I agreed to eat dinner in the
kitchen together, like we had done a thousand times before.

We listened to "Nazi Eyes on Canada" on the radio
for as long as we could handle hearing about Hitler's
plans for world domination. I flipped the switch, turning
the show off. I had had enough violence to last a lifetime.

We agreed to read to each other from *Life Magazine*,
where we could pick and chose what we wanted to hear.

We read about society weddings and other stories not war related. If Anca noticed that I had taken to carrying the shotgun with me, and had propped it against the wall near the refectory table where we sat, she didn't let on. We read and talked, reminiscing about old times, until we were both ready for bed. Anca stood up from the table and bid me good night. She went to pick up the tray that was littered with our tea cups, saucers, and the now empty plate which had been piled high with my favorite cookies.

"I'll take care of that," I said.

She smiled at me and said good night once more, for the last time. Tomorrow she would leave us for good.

"Will you please lock your door tonight?"

"Yes." She didn't ask me why I requested this. She trusted me enough to comply without question.

I cleaned up our dishes and, with my shotgun in tow, went upstairs to bed.

Zeke should be back from the airport by now. What was taking him so long? Unable to sleep, afraid of the things I couldn't see, I put on warm clothes and kept a restless vigil by my open window, hoping all the while that Zeke would return soon.

Hours went by. Zeke did not appear. It must have been around midnight when I decided to make myself some hot cocoa. I closed the window, pulled the blackout curtains tight, and lit the candle by my bed. I decided against bringing the shotgun downstairs with me, knowing full well that I couldn't shoot someone while carrying cocoa. In the kitchen, the open curtains allowed the moon to cast her glow on the old flagstone floor. Outside the oleander swayed, the moonlight shimmered on its leaves like silvery filigree. Using my candle, I lit the gas stove, and turned the blue flame on high. I had just taken one of the copper pans off the shelf when a figure dressed in dark clothing crept across the back lawn toward the woods. Without thinking, I turned off the stove, blew out my candle, and headed into the night.

Vivian, with her fashionable hair style, her well-groomed feet, and closet full of elegant clothes, didn't strike me as someone who would spend her free time trekking through the woods, messing up her hair and smudging her makeup. She knew the path that wove parallel to the beach and took it tonight, with only the moon to light her way.

I followed her, knowing that we would wind up in town, avoiding the beach proper. She left the safety of the trees and shrubs and stepped onto the main street, behind the post office. She headed toward the community center, a non-descript wooden building, painted white, with a shale roof that was forever in need of repair. Tonight a dance was in full swing. I recognized a Benny Goodman tune and wondered at the live dance band in Bennett Cove.

On first glance, the blacked-out community center windows made the building appear dark and desolate, but the sound of the orchestra and the people who milled about outside revealed the buzz of activity that took place inside. I could see Vivian now. She dashed into some bushes and, in a matter of seconds, stepped out of them dressed in a sky-blue silk dress and off-white high heels. Her metamorphosis was remarkable. There was no evidence of her trek on foot from Bennett House. She came out of those bushes looking like she had been driven to town by a chauffeur. Rather than going in to the dance, she walked past the front door and into the darkened alley on the side of the building. I marveled at her professionalism as I followed her, ducking along in the shadows and using the bushes for cover. A series of waste bins were lined up near the door by the community center's kitchen. I ducked behind them and watched my stepmother as she approached a man dressed in civilian clothes.

The band was too loud for me to hear what they were saying, but by some fortuitous coincidence, the musicians took their break, and I was able to hear every word of Vivian's clandestine tryst. The man she met was not a love interest. She kept too much of a distance for any intimacy. When he stepped close to her, perhaps so they wouldn't be overheard, she stepped away, as if she didn't trust him. He was shorter than she, which wasn't saying much, because she was a tall woman. The man to whom she spoke was dressed like a dock worker, with a tattered pea coat, a dark knit cap, and heavy corduroy trousers—

common working attire for the men who made their living catching fish in the waters off Bennett Cove, the same fishermen who now went out with radar—provided by the military—to look for submarines.

His shoes gave him away. The shiny black oxfords were polished to such a high shine the moonbeams bounced off them. These were not the shoes of a dock worker or a fisherman. They were city shoes. I crept behind the waste bins, moving closer to where they stood.

Vivian handed the man the satchel that she had carried. "Here's the film."

He took it from her and said something that I couldn't hear.

"But you were supposed to bring me money," she said. "I need it tonight."

The man mumbled something back to her, but I couldn't hear it.

"Don't you double-cross me." Her voice became agitated and took on that shrill quality that rankled. The man shrugged as he stepped away from her. She reached out to grab him, but he was too quick.

"Stupid dame," he said as he pushed her, knocking her off balance. He fled into the cover of darkness behind the community center. She stumbled and almost fell, but at the last minute she righted herself. Vivian took a moment to regain her composure, after which she walked right past me. She slipped into the bushes and out of sight.

I could only guess what had just transpired, or where Vivian was headed now.

I had stepped out from my hiding place behind the garbage cans, ready to follow Vivian back through the bushes and take the trail back to Bennett House when three men came around the side of the building. They stumbled as they walked and sang bawdy songs in their loud drunken voices. They passed a bottle of booze, each tipping his head back as he drank.

"Excuse me." I attempted to pass but one of the men grabbed my arm.

"Where do you think you're going, sweetheart?" He pulled me near him, his grip vice-like on my arm. His friends moved closer, encircling me, blocking my passage.

I tried to pull away. The more I fought, the deeper his fingers dug into my flesh. He jerked my wrist so hard an electrical jolt of pain ran up my arm and into my shoulder. My heart started to pound. No one knew I was here. No one would come to my rescue. I was on my own.

I couldn't overcome these men. They circled around me, leering, their eyes glassy from booze, their faces hardened and mean.

I screamed as loud as I could, "Fire!"

"What the—"

When I screamed, the man loosened his grip just enough for me to break free. I took off running, not looking back to see whether or not they followed. My heart pounded hard and fast, ready to explode, but still I ran. If I could make it to the front of the building where other people milled about, smoking cigarettes and stepping outside as the band took their break, someone would help me.

I would find a policeman, anyone, who could see me home. I was just about to turn the corner, when I ran right into Zeke's arms.

I hit him with such velocity, we almost went flying, but Zeke, by some miracle, managed to stay on his feet and keep me standing up as well. His arms went around me. The last of my composure slipped away and, in the safety of his arms, I crumpled and wept the loud racking sobs guaranteed to make my nose run and swell into a red bulb. I was not a pretty woman after a spate of tears.

I didn't know how long Zeke held me. He didn't let go until I stopped crying and calmed my breathing.

"Come on, let's get you home." He kept his arm around me, encircling me with the heat of his body as we walked toward the car.

We didn't speak much during the ride home, but Zeke held my hand, maintaining the connection between us, and not letting go until we pulled up to the front door of Bennett House. The house was quiet and still from the outside, but inside firelight from the library welcomed us. He helped me with my coat. After he hung it on one of the hooks by the front door, he took my hand and led me into the library. I sat on the couch while Zeke got a blanket and draped it around my shoulders.

Anca came in carrying a tray with mugs of cocoa, along with a plate of cookies and ham sandwiches.

"What were you doing tonight, out there in a dark alley all by yourself? You know better than that. I've met naïve women before, but really, Sarah, you—"

"I found microfilm in her room."

"You what? When?"

"Yesterday, I caught her in my father's desk, snooping, and discovered later that my passport and birth certificate were missing. When she got in the bath, I searched her room. I wanted my papers back."

"What did you do with the film?" he asked.

"Put it back. I knew she'd miss it, and I knew that you were aware of it, so I thought that it was best to just leave it."

"Thank God," Zeke said.

"You're glad I put the film back?"

"I've been switching her film since I started working for your father."

"So all this time—"

"She's been passing along inaccurate information," Zeke said. "And I have reason to believe the people that she has been passing the film to know that I've been switching it. That's why she's anxious to leave town. If Vivian is no longer of value to these people, they won't hesitate to get her out of the way."

"Where is she now? She's not here, is she?"

"No," Zeke said. "I came home. Anca was awake. I went upstairs to make sure you were locked in your room, but the door was open and you were gone. Vivian was also gone, so I assumed the worst and came looking for you. It was just dumb luck that I happened to walk around that corner when I did."

"You saved me once again."

"What were you doing out there by yourself?"

"Following Vivian," I said. "She wants to leave here and she needs money."

"I need you to tell me exactly what you saw tonight. Can you describe the person Vivian met? Did you hear anything they said?" Zeke proceeded to ask questions about the minute details of Vivian's encounter with the man in the alley. His questions were designed to jog my memory. When I told him about the incongruous shoes, Zeke smiled, as if pleased with my attention to detail. He sat next to me, quiet, his brow furrowed in concentration.

"I'm not going to leave you alone anymore. It's no longer safe."

I didn't argue with him.

"I need to say something to you. When I said that I couldn't get involved—well, I think that is a decision that you should be involved in. My future is uncertain. I have obligations, which may require me to leave you alone for long periods of time. Not many women would want to live like that. I can't make any real commitments, ask you to marry me, until I finish some things that I cannot explain to you. I don't feel right asking you to wait."

"I'll wait for you," I whispered.

He pulled me close and kissed me, a stop-the-world kiss that told me everything I needed to know. Then we leaned back, our bodies close as we stared into the fire.

"She's going to assume my identity. That's why she took my documents—my passport and birth certificate. She's looking for the money to leave Bennett Cove. She's going to travel as Sarah Bennett."

"I won't let that happen," Zeke said.

I believed him.

# CHAPTER 15

Despite the madness of the previous night, I awoke early the next morning, refreshed and rejuvenated. I had been kissed. I was in love. I got out of bed and pulled open the curtains, to be greeted by fog thick as mud and just as opaque. I didn't care. With a song in my heart, I dressed with care and dabbed some lipstick on before going downstairs for breakfast.

Anca was in the kitchen, pulling a tray of biscuits out of the oven. I poured myself tea from the pot and added milk. I took the biscuits that had just come out of the oven off the cookie sheet and set them on the cooling rack.

"Where's Viv—Grace?" I asked, trying to make my voice sound light and uninterested.

"She was gone when I turned her room. I hate to

leave you alone with that woman. I knew she was trouble the first time I saw her." She came to me and grabbed my arm. "You must be very careful when I am gone. Let your young man protect you. She is dangerous." She made the cross over her chest. "Zeke is getting the car ready to take me to town. He told me to keep an eye on you until he gets back."

"I'm going to miss you, Anca."

"He's in love with you." Anca waited for me to look at her and tell her what had happened between us, but I didn't. I moved over to the kitchen window and ate my biscuit, holding it over the sink as I did so. "You've found out that you were adopted, haven't you?"

"You knew?"

"I'm sorry to have kept it from you. I gave my word to your grandmother that I would never tell you about your adoption. I'm so very sorry for everything that you have had to go through, Sarah—Jessica's death, the asylum."

"It's not your fault."

"You've seen her, haven't you?" Anca asked.

"I've seen her spirit."

"You always could see through the veil, even when you were little. Do you remember having tea with Esther Bennett?"

Esther Bennet had been dead for decades, but her reputation lived on. Legend had it that she won fifty acres of our family's land in a game of cards. When she went to the man's house to collect the deed, he tried to back out of paying her. The poor man made the mistake of saying that a simpleminded woman could never win a card game. He then was stupid enough to tell her to go home where she belonged and stay in her place. She pulled a gun on him and held it there until he signed the necessary paperwork to transfer the land to her. I didn't remember having tea with her, I'm sorry to say.

"Your parents weren't happy, that I can tell you. She told you some interesting things which you repeated to your parents. Of course, they rationalized it, said that you simply overheard them speaking."

"Why did you never speak to me about this before?"

"Because this ability you have is something that you must learn to accept and deal with on your own." She picked up a cloth and started wiping the counters. "These things come and go. You may see your real mother's spirit now, and then you may not ever see it again. It's best not to make too much of it, better just to let things happen in their own good time. You could be seeing your mother for a special reason. There is no bond greater than that of a mother and child."

"She must want something from me."

"Or you might need something from her. Only time will tell."

We hugged.

"I'm going to miss you," I said for the hundredth time.

"I will be close. You can visit. Now we work."

And work we did. Anca made sure I knew where everything was kept, how to lay the trays for morning, the best way to bake the bread, clean the larder, and de-frost the icebox.

She showed me the easiest way to do the laundry, fold the sheets so they wouldn't wrinkle, and a myriad of other tasks.

Hours later, just as we were finished cleaning up the kitchen, after baking enough bread to last a few days, fingers of sunlight broke through the fog. My arms ached and my hands were blistered. Soon Zeke would be back. Together we would drive Anca to the bus stop in town.

After Anca wiped the kitchen counter for the last time, she hung the dish towel on the hook and stood surveying the room that she had claimed as her own these past years. "Will you get my suitcase for me from the attic?"

"Of course."

She retreated to her bedroom to start packing.

On my way upstairs, I detoured into my father's office. The top of the desk had been cleared before his trip. All that remained was a lone piece of paper with the phone number for the Algonquin Hotel that sat on top of the desk. I picked up the phone and asked the operator to put me through to the Algonquin Hotel.

"Is this a necessary long distance call?"

"Yes, it is. I'll be brief."

"Thank you for helping keep the phone lines clear for the war effort. Connecting."

After three or four rings, the clerk at the Algonquin answered. I asked to be connected to my father's room.

"One moment, please."

She put me on hold, and it seemed like ages before she came back.

"Mr. Bennett is not here," she said.

I left a message, asking him to call home. He needed to know what was going on here. I owed him that. I walked over to Zeke's desk and stood over it for a moment, thinking of him sitting here, reading this book, touching that ink well, and resting his elbow on this blotter.

The hairs on the back of my neck and my arms stood up, as a draft came through the room. I shivered, overcome by the feeling that I was not alone. I turned and took in my surroundings to assure myself that no one had followed me into the room. I was ready to chastise myself for being paranoid, but the heavy velvet curtain rustled, as if someone were behind it, which was impossible, since the house was still locked up from the night before. I went over to the window and pushed the curtain aside. It was open. I reached over to shut it again, just as Vivian headed across the lawn and onto the trail up the mountain. She was also in disguise, and just as Zeke had said, she had changed her appearance with an expertise that I had to admire. She even managed to change the way she moved. Her face and hair were hidden by a navy scarf and a huge pair of sun glasses. She seemed taller somehow, and I wondered if she wore special shoes to disguise her height.

*Where in the world is she going?*

Throwing the first coat I could grab over my shoulders, I followed her as she hurried up the steep and twisty path to the cabins on the hill. She navigated the rough terrain like a mountain goat, once again surprising me with her physical prowess. The day was clear and cold, with a good ocean breeze to blow the morning fog away. The trees danced to the music of the wind in their canopy above me, hiding the sound of my breath as I labored to keep up with her and muffling the sound of the loose stones that went rolling down the footpath in my wake.

I stopped in my tracks. I had been so lost in thought that I had traveled a good half mile from the house, which was out of sight now. The only sound was the wind in the trees and the crying of the gulls as they circled above me. I was alone, far away from anyone, on the heels of a cunning, murderous spy. What was I thinking, following this woman? What was I going to do if I caught her in the act, up here, by myself? Hadn't Zeke asked me not to do anything foolish? Hadn't Anca promised him that she would keep me out of trouble?

I turned around and headed back to the house, weaving my way down the path, every now and then stopping to take in the view of the Pacific Ocean. I had marveled at this view a million times, yet it was so spectacular that I once again stopped and took in the beauty. There were no boats near the shore today. I could almost pretend that we weren't at war, that the threat of enemy invasion wasn't imminent.

I leaned against a giant redwood tree and tilted my face toward the sun. Was Vivian going up the mountain to send a radio signal to her ring of spies? No matter. I was helpless to do anything about it. I pushed away from the tree and was about to continue the hike down the hill toward Bennett House when something whizzed by my ear, brushed against my hair, then thumped against the tree trunk.

A knot formed in my stomach. It started out as fear, but blossomed into rage when I saw the knife embedded in the tree not three inches from where I had just been leaning. Had I not moved, it would have landed in my neck. The knife was wedged up to its hilt in the trunk of the tree that I had leaned on. Vivian was nowhere to be seen, at least not from where I stood.

Grabbing the slick, colorful handle, I wrenched the embedded knife out of the tree and studied it. It was exactly like the one I had found in my father's desk drawer, like the knife that had killed Gran. Bright stripes of yellow, red, purple, and green decorated the handle. I ran my finger along the shiny steel blade. It sliced through my skin. A tiny trickle of my blood seeped out of the small wound.

I took my handkerchief and wrapped the knife in it then tucked the bundle in my pocket. I applied pressure to the small cut I had made, until it stopped bleeding. Then I continued on the path toward safety, moving as quickly as I could without tumbling.

Vivian Mason had just tried to kill me.

# CHAPTER 16

The baking we had done earlier left the kitchen warm and sweet smelling. It was too early for the morning sun to filter through the windows, so oil lamps were still lit, giving the room an even cozier feeling. The heat stung my wind-burnt cheeks as I came through the door. Anca and Zeke were sitting at the kitchen table. Anca had been crying, tears ran down her cheeks, and she dabbed at them with a handkerchief, the lace around its edges yellowed with age. Her rosary lay on the table before her. Zeke sat close to her. He had one arm around her shoulder, and spoke to her in a soft comforting manner. When Anca saw me, she made the sign of the cross over her chest.

"Thank you, God," she said. She picked up her rosary, her fingers running along the beads with the dexterity of a concert pianist, her lips moving as she prayed, the handkerchief she held waving like a flag of surrender.

"Where have you been?" Zeke asked.

"Why are you crying?" I asked Anca.

"She's been worried about you," Zeke said. "Didn't we agree that you wouldn't do anything foolish like go off on your own?"

I hadn't noticed before how Zeke's face had become gaunt, his complexion pale. He had been pushing himself too hard. "I promised I wouldn't leave you alone, promised I would keep you safe." Anca wiped her eyes. "When I came back into the kitchen, you were gone. I didn't know where you went. I was afraid someone had taken you against your will."

"I'm sorry I upset you, Anca."

"You're fine, so it was nothing. I am a nervous old woman." She pushed away from the table. "I'll think I'll rest for a while."

"I'll get your suitcase," I said.

Anca went down the hall to her room. When Zeke and I were alone, I pulled the knife wrapped in my father's handkerchief out of my jacket pocket and set it on the table.

"What's that?" Zeke asked.

"I followed Vivian Mason up the hill toward the cabins." I looked at Zeke, met his eyes, and held them. "I was halfway there when I remembered what you told me about keeping myself safe, so I turned around and was headed home, proud of myself for not being a fool. I stopped for a second to enjoy the view and was leaning against a tree when she threw that at me." I nodded toward the white handkerchief, the familiar JB monogram on the corner.

Zeke unwrapped the bundle, situating the knife on top of my father's handkerchief. He didn't touch it. He hovered over it until his face was inches from it.

"You say Vivian Mason threw this at you?"

"Yes," I said. "She left the house and I followed her."

"You're sure it was her?"

"Of course, I'm sure. Black hair, tall, lives here. Yes, it was her."

Zeke shook his head. "That's impossible."

"What do you mean? I followed her."

"I just don't see how—"

"I'm telling you, I saw her with my own eyes. She left this house and I followed her."

"She rode into town with me, Sarah. I had errands to run and she asked for a ride. There's no way she was the one you followed, unless she is able to be in two places at once."

"What?"

"There's no way she could have made it back here, then up the trail to the cabins. It's virtually impossible," Zeke said.

"But I don't understand." I pulled out a chair and sat down at the table. There were so many facts, so many nuggets of information spinning around in my head, that I couldn't keep everything straight. If it wasn't Vivian, who in the world had I followed?

Zeke sat down next to me. When he pulled me into his arms, I shivered and leaned into him, savoring the feel of his body next to mine. "We need to hurry if we are going to get Anca to the bus on time," he whispered into my ear.

"I'm going to get Anca's suitcase. I'll be right back, okay?"

"Sure. I'll just wait right here."

Zeke's exhaustion kept him from propriety. He didn't stand up when I left the room. When I turned back to look at him, he had folded his arms on the kitchen table and cradled his head in them. I watched him there, still and quiet, until his breathing became regular and deep. He was asleep.

I left him there.

℘ℑℰℑ

The third-floor attic had the most natural light and the best view of any room in Bennett House. Leaded windows graced all four walls. The floor was constructed of wide-planked wood. The white-washed walls made the room seem bright, even if the sun wasn't shining. Anca

never came up here—she had listened to too many of
Mrs. Tolliver's ghost stories. Mrs. Tolliver was a great
one for telling tall tales about mysterious goings on at
Bennett House. I ignored the stories of witches and demons, just like I ignored the children that teased me, just
like I ignored the mothers who pulled them out of my
path. Anca, on the other hand, would not walk under lad-
ders, own a black cat, or go anywhere where spirits might
reside. She slept with garlic under her pillow, and vases
of flowers and herbs strategically placed around her room
for protection. Despite the random junk accumulated over
the decades, the attic was arranged with some semblance
of order. In one corner, old furniture, some broken and
unusable, some dated or no longer necessary—like our
old washboard that should have been thrown out when
we purchased our washing machine, and a dozen old tin
milk cans, now rusty and covered with dust—were
stacked against a wall. Next to them, boxes of my grandfather's papers were stored, waiting for my father to go
through them and write our family history—his family's
history, rather. The suitcases and trunks were on the opposite wall, stacked one on top of the other.

Anca's suitcase, a faded cloth valise that was probably as old as she was, lay next to a pile of trunks. One of
the trunks that I had never seen before caught my eye. It
was made of fine wood, with polished brass hinges and
an impenetrable iron lock. My heart pounded as I read the
name tag which hung on the front of it. Grace Kensing-

ton, my mother. Vivian had stolen this from her, had taken it out of the house before she had burnt it down.

On a whim, I moved the trunk away from the wall and tried the latch, hoping that it wouldn't be locked. It wasn't. I lifted the lid and the scent of cedar assaulted my senses, fresh and clean as a spring day. An old hand knit woolen sweater lay rumpled in one corner. I held it up, taking in the missing buttons and the moth hole in the collar. I sneezed and set the sweater aside. Nestled in the corner lay a leather pouch shaped like an envelope.

"Sarah," Anca called from the bottom of the stairs, "I am ready for my case."

"Coming," I said, as I grabbed the pouch and closed the trunk, careful to put it back as I had found it. On my way downstairs, I did a quick detour to my room, where I stored the pouch under my bed, tucked well up in the box-spring, just in case Vivian came snooping.

附

The fog had burned off by the time Zeke and I had Anca and her valise loaded into the car. I was amazed that she had so little to take with her. Other than her coat, a utilitarian gray wool affair, and her two hats, one for church and one for every day, her little valise held all she needed in the world.

"You'll be sure and tell Mrs. Tolliver to bring eggs every other week," Anca said.

When we pulled up to the station, a long line of soldiers had queued up for the bus to San Francisco. We got out of the car. Zeke handed Anca the valise, gave her a quick hug, and left us alone.

"All aboard," the bus driver said, as he moved down the line, taking the tickets.

"May God be with you, Sarah Jane," she whispered in my ear as she hugged me. "I will pray for you every day."

"Thanks." I pulled away and smiled at her.

"Anca, Anca," Mrs. Tolliver called out, waving one arm as she hurried over to us. She carried a small burlap bag, similar to the one she had with her on the bus the day I had come home. "I've brought you some vegetable soup."

"Bless you." Anca took the bag and tucked it under her arm.

"I won't say good bye," Mrs. Tolliver said.

Anca smiled. She waved to both of us and boarded the bus. Mrs. Tolliver and I stood shoulder to shoulder until the last soldier boarded, the doors closed with a whoosh, and the bus pulled away.

"That was nice of you to come and say goodbye," I said to Mrs. Tolliver.

"So you know." Mrs. Tolliver studied my face.

"Know what?"

"You've discovered you can see beyond the veil. We've known all along, but Anca told me not to speak of it." She grabbed my hand in her cold dry one, pulled me close, and looked me in the eyes. "You have a friend in me, Sarah. You fight when you need to."

"I need to go, Mrs. Tolliver." I pulled out of her strong grasp and pointed to Zeke, who now had the car idling. "He's waiting for me."

"You can't deny it, girl," she said. "You can't deny what God gave you."

"You take care, Mrs. Tolliver."

# CHAPTER 17

Zeke got out of the driver's side of the car, and, always a gentleman, opened the door for me. He settled himself behind the wheel. "Who was that lady you were talking to?"

"Mrs. Tolliver, Bennett Cove's resident witch, fortune teller, and all around eccentric."

Zeke put the car in gear and headed away from the bus stop. Rather than driving home, he continued down Main Street two blocks to the Sand Dollar. Famous for their clam chowder and fresh seafood, the Sand Dollar also made fabulous hamburgers. As we pulled up to the café, a car pulled out of the parking place a short distance from the café. Zeke maneuvered my father's Studebaker into the spot.

"I'll be right back," he said.

The Sand Dollar had a crowd of soldiers and civilians alike waiting for a table. Many sat on the benches in front of the restaurant, others stood in groups. Zeke said hello to a few of the men standing around outside. They smiled and waved at him. One man clapped Zeke on the back and shook his hand. Zeke cast a glance in my direction, then slipped into the restaurant.

A sharp knock on the passenger window pulled me out of my reverie. A woman with a friendly face smiled at me as I rolled down the window.

"Sarah, my name is Cynthia Forrester. I am a writer—"

I started to roll up the window.

"Wait. Please. Just listen." She slipped her card through the window. "If you ever want me to write a story from your point of view, call that number. I am willing to sign a contract, giving you full right to edit anything before it goes to print. If you want to tell your story, I hope you'll call me. I won't bother you again."

She stood up and walked away. I was so busy watching her that I almost didn't notice the black sedan I had seen on my first day home, and later at the hotel. It turned into the alleyway next to the cafe. Zeke's contact. A uniformed chauffeur got out and opened the back door for the man I recognized from the Bennett Arms. He got out of the car, walked toward the restaurant, and reached the door just as Zeke came out. Zeke pulled the paper bag containing our food close to his chest before he cast a swift glance at my direction.

They stepped out of earshot of the crowd gathered around the front door of the café. The man spoke to Zeke, conveying an authority that I could sense without hearing their conversation. Zeke listened to him, focused on his every word. He mouthed something back—I would have given anything to hear the conversation—then he looked at me, an uncomfortable expression etched on his face.

A few seconds later, Zeke got in the car, handed me the bag of food and sped out of the parking lot.

"Who was that man? He looks familiar."

"I don't know. I've never seen him before." Zeke lied with ease. "He was just asking directions." He pulled an expert U-turn, then headed back to Bennett House.

"If this is going to work, you're going to have to be honest with me. I saw you talking to that very same man in the hotel a couple of days ago, and on the day I came home."

Zeke was just about to turn onto the twisty road that wound up the hill to Bennett House. He pulled over on the narrow dirt shoulder, put the car in park, and turned to face me. "Okay, here's the truth. He's the man who hired me to find your mother. He needs to remain anonymous because he works for the FBI. He's here to make sure Vivian Mason doesn't get away. I can't tell you anything else."

"But I have a right—"

"You don't," Zeke interrupted. "You don't have a right to know. I've told you too much already. Please. Just trust me." He kissed my forehead, put the car in gear, and pulled back onto the road headed toward Bennett House.

"What are you thinking about?" Zeke asked as he drove, keeping his eyes on the road.

"French fries, and my stepmother—Vivian Mason, or whoever she is." My stomach growled. "If it wasn't Vivian who I followed this morning, who was it?" We were now on the gravel road that led to Bennett House. "Do you think that Vivian could have snuck back here? Maybe she had an accomplice drive her. You know, it's a perfect alibi, since as far as you're concerned, there's no way she could have made it back in time."

"Something's not right. It seems like we aren't seeing something that is right under our nose," Zeke said.

We took our food into the kitchen and ate at the refectory table. After we finished, Zeke threw away our paper wrappers, and wiped our crumbs away.

"Do you want to get a book and sit in the office with me while I work?"

I frowned at him.

"Don't look at me that way. Someone threw a knife at you today. I meant it when I said I'm not leaving you alone anymore."

"But even in the house—"

"Especially in this house."

I leaned against the chopping table in the middle of the kitchen, the same table where Anca and I had rolled out bread dough just a few hours ago. Zeke came over and stood close to me. I wrapped my arms around him.

"It's important that you have as little interaction with Vivian Mason as possible. She's dangerous, Sarah, ergo you will not be alone with her. Okay? I don't mean to sound bossy. I just don't want anything to happen to you."

Together we walked into the office, arm in arm. Once we were inside, Zeke closed and locked the door behind us.

He pulled a folder out of the leather folio that he carried with him all the time. He unfolded a series of strange looking maps and spread them out on his desk. He sat down and started to study them, and it didn't take long for him to become so engrossed in his task that he all but forgot about me.

I paced around the room for a minute, sat down, and tried to read, but I couldn't concentrate. "I think I'll go to my room."

"Hang on." Zeke put the maps back in the folio, which he in turn tucked under his arm. "I'll walk you upstairs." He smiled as he placed his hand on the small of my back. In his free hand he carried the shotgun. "Lock the door behind you." When we came to my bedroom door, he handed me the shotgun. "And keep this with you."

I did as he asked, standing on the other side of the door as he shook it to test the lock.

"Are you okay, Sarah?"

"I'm fine," I said through the door. "I'm going to bathe and change my clothes. I'll be down in an hour or so."

"We need to keep our heads on straight, Sarah. I need to stay focused, and so do you."

I didn't say anything.

"Just keep the door locked, and I'll be downstairs if you need me."

As soon as Zeke's footsteps faded away, I pulled the leather pouch I had found in Grace's trunk from its hiding place. I sat on my bed, opened it, and emptied its contents onto the counterpane.

Two passports tumbled onto my bed. They both had blue leather covers and gold embossed lettering on the front. My hands started to shake. I opened the passport. Inside, the spot where the picture should have been was empty. The pages of my mother's passport were filled with stamps from other countries. I recognized Switzerland, Italy, Germany, all places she had visited in the past. My own passport and birth certificate were at the bottom of the pile, along with a bank book from First Bank of Maine. I opened the bank book, surprised at the great sum of money on deposit.

A locket, exactly like that which Grace wore around her neck, wedged itself in the bottom of the envelope. I took it out and held it in my hand, remembering Grace's words as though she whispered them in my ear. *It holds a picture of my husband and daughter.* She would clutch the locket while she said these words, a wistful smile on her face. With shaking hands I undid the catch and opened the locket. Inside was a picture of me as a baby. I had never seen any baby pictures of myself, but I knew that red-headed child, with the ringlets that couldn't be tamed and the dimpled face, was me. I was in the arms of a tall, lean, athletic-looking man with the type of Patrician nose that one often sees in old portraits of kings and lords.

Although the picture was somewhat faded, the man had dark hair, sad brooding eyes, and strong muscular arms. I imagined he played polo or jumped horses over tall fences.

I guessed that the man in the photo was my biological father, but I didn't share the same gut wrenching connection to this man that I shared with Grace Kensington.

A picture of her as a young girl was on the other side of the locket. I stared at it until my eyes hurt. I closed the locket, attached the chain around my neck, and tucked it under my blouse, where it rested out of sight, but near my heart. I focused on the other passport that had fallen out of the leather pouch.

This one didn't have any gold letters on the front of it. Inside, the pages were similar to the passport that had belonged to my mother, but the interior paper was a little off color and not quite the same thickness as my mother's original passport. This passport was a forgery.

Eager to share what I had found with Zeke, I put the passports back in the leather pouch and headed downstairs, not bothering to bring the shotgun with me.

I knocked on the office door, which was closed and locked. I heard papers rustling, a drawer opening and shutting. "It's just me."

"What's happened?" Zeke opened the door and searched my face. "You look like you've had a shock."

I went into the office and sat down at Zeke's desk. The maps had been stowed away, so he didn't lock the door behind me.

After I sat, he went over to the credenza behind my father's desk and poured some scotch in a glass for me. I took the drink from him and handed him the leather pouch.

He sat down on the corner of the desk and opened it. He took out my passport and birth certificate and set them aside. He picked up the other two passports and examined them thoroughly before he put them back in the pouch. He took out the bank book, studied it, and put it back in the pouch with the passports.

"Where did you find this?"

"In the attic. I stumbled across it when I retrieved Anca's suitcase. There's also this." I reached under my blouse for the locket. I tried to undo the clasp, but my hands had started shaking.

Zeke came around behind me. I held my hair up.
When his fingers touched the back of my neck, a shiver
ran down my spine. He held the necklace up before him.
The gold locket swung like a pendulum and shone like a
beacon. He opened it. "These are you parents."

I nodded.

"I'm glad you have this memento." He closed the
locket, and I once again held up my hair so he could affix
the clasp. He kissed the back of my neck before he turned
me around to face him. When we were face to face, he
hugged me. I leaned in and tipped my face up to him for
the inevitable kiss. Our lips had almost touched, when the
front door opened. Vivian was home.

"Just act natural, okay?" Zeke whispered in my ear.
In one smooth movement, he unlocked the desk drawer,
swept the leather pouch containing the passports into it,
closed it, and locked it.

Vivian swept into the room. She had on trousers and
walking shoes. Her hair was covered by a beige silk scarf
with blue flowers embroidered throughout. She carried a
basket on her arm, which contained a loaf of bread and a
jar of jam, which I recognized to be Mrs. Tolliver's.

"Drinking this early?" Vivian walked over to my father's desk and set the basket down on the desktop. She
sat down in his chair and opened the desk drawer.

Neither Zeke nor I said anything while Vivian took
out the big checkbook, opened it, and wrote a check with
the fountain pen that lay on top of the desk. She signed

her name with a flourish. When she had finished writing, she looked at me. "Don't worry, Sarah. I'm just getting some money for household expenses. Now that Anca's gone, someone has to do the shopping."

"Of course, thank you."

"What's happened?" Her eyes swept from Zeke to me. "Why are you both acting so strangely?"

Zeke stood, thank God, as I was unable to.

"Someone threw a knife at Sarah this morning. As you can imagine, she's had quite a shock."

"Are you all right?" Vivian's concern seemed natural, as if she cared what happened to me, as if she were surprised at the unfortunate attempt on my life.

"I'll be fine."

She turned around and with her back to us, fiddled with the crystal decanter and the glasses on the credenza. When she turned around, she had two glasses of scotch in her hands. She stood and brought one over to Zeke. She kept the other one for herself.

"To calm nerves," she said, after we all had glasses in our hands.

I lifted the glass to my lips, so did Zeke. He took a sip, and threw the glass to the floor where it shattered on the hard wood.

"Sarah..." Zeke took a few steps toward Vivian, staggered, and fell to the floor.

"Zeke," I cried out. I set my drink down and ran over to him.

Vivian picked up Zeke's glass, surveying the liquid that remained.

"What did you give him?" I shouted at her.

"Just a little something. I'm not going to tell you until you give me your passport and birth certificate. I need them, so I can leave here. If you cooperate with me, I'll tell you what I've given Zeke so the doctor can fix him."

I knelt down next to Zeke. He trembled and clutched his chest as he beckoned me to bend close to him.

"I'm okay. Get her out of here and I'll call the police," he whispered in my ear.

"What did he just say?" Vivian stood behind me, staring down at Zeke. "What did he just say to you?"

"He told me to give you what you want." I stood up.

"Then I suggest you do it. Get the passports," she said. "And be quick about it."

I raced up the stairs, into my room, grateful for the shotgun that rested against the wall where I had left it. Vivian followed behind me, step for step. I slammed the door shut and had almost slid the lock in place, but I wasn't quick enough. Vivian threw her weight against the door and barged into the room.

The force of the door opening knocked me off my feet. I landed on my bottom, using my wrists to break the fall. Pain shot up my arm. I scrambled to get away from her, backing myself into the corner. I lunged for the shotgun, but she got there before me. With a stoic precision that made my blood run cold, Vivian took the two shells out of the gun and put them in her pocket. She leaned the gun against the wall with exaggerated nonchalance, as if she were propping up something innocuous, like an old ladder or a broken chair.

"There now," she said, as she moved to stand in the doorway, blocking any attempt I might make to get away from her.

"You killed my mother. You stole her trunk, her clothes, her jewelry. You allowed those women to burn alive." My voice was hysterical and shrill.

"What do you care, Sarah? You never even knew her. You want me to feel sorry for you, with your privileged life? Do you realize how foolish you are? And you can wipe that smug look off your face. You don't think Zeke is interested in anything but your money, do you?" She moved close to bend down, bringing her face so close to me I could see a tiny blue vein bulge on her forehead and smell her foul breath. "None of that matters now. I'm leaving this hole of a town, and let me tell you, I can't get out of here fast enough," she said.

"You'll never get away with it."

"Of course, I will."

"Not if I tell—" I wouldn't be doing any telling. She was going to kill me, in cold blood, like she had killed my mother.

"Now you understand. Good. That makes it easier. Dying isn't so bad, Sarah. I'll do it so it doesn't hurt, like I did your mother and your great-aunt. You'll be glad to know that I put knock-out drops in their coffee. I didn't start the fire until they were fast asleep. And since you're being so cooperative, I'll tell you about your mother. She was coming to find you, her long lost daughter, whom she loved with a quiet desperation that made me sick."

"Why did you kill her?" I tried to keep my voice calm, tried to keep Vivian talking.

"Don't try to distract me, Sarah. This is business for me. I'm a professional. So if you're thinking in that tiny brain of yours that you might be able to thwart me and come out of this situation victorious, think again. This little thing between us—" She waved her hand around my room. "—this is nothing to me. I'll kill you, and move on. As for your mother, she discovered who I was when I tried to withdraw some money out of her bank account in Maine. That woman had the audacity to search my things. She found some pictures I had taken that would have secured my financial future. I had to stop her before she ruined everything that I've worked so hard to attain. If she hadn't meddled, I wouldn't be here. I wouldn't have to kill you."

"Zeke knows who you are," I said. "He's going to track you down. You'll hang for treason."

She laughed. "You naïve idiot. Zeke is going to die. I gave him enough digitalis to kill a horse."

"You killed Gran, too," I said.

"Of course I didn't. Don't be stupid. Your grandmother was a meddling fool but she never did anything to me. You don't seem to realize that things change when a war is on." She pushed away from me. "Maybe I'll burn Bennett House to the ground. Wouldn't that be a triumph?"

The dark bubble of hatred that had been simmering since I came home, boiled over. Like a wild animal, I launched myself at her. It seemed that I watched a film as it ran in slow motion. Vivian's face took on a sudden look of surprise; her eyebrows raised, her mouth formed a perfect "O."

I crashed into her with such force that we tumbled through the open bedroom door and onto the landing. Vivian recovered, came at me again, this time flipping us, with her atop me. She grabbed a thick lock of my hair and yanked. My rage rendered me impervious to the pain. Vivian stood up, and, with a surprising show of strength, she pulled me up with her. I charged again, throwing all my weight against her. The momentum of my body and the speed with which I threw myself hurtled us toward the railing.

The banister splintered before it collapsed under our weight. Together we plummeted downward, our fall broken by the wooden table in the foyer. The table shattered. We both hit the ground with a thud. I got a quick glimpse of the surprise frozen on Vivian's face. Then everything went black.

# CHAPTER 18

When I woke up, Sheriff Carpenter stood over me. At first I didn't remember what had happened. A hazy fog enshrouded everything and wouldn't allow me to focus. The white hairs in Sheriff Carpenter's nose were thick and luxurious. I giggled as I tried to sit up, but when I put weight on my arm, bright lights flashed before my eyes and a wave of nausea washed over me.

"She's awake," Sheriff Carpenter said.

"Zeke." I thought I cried out, but my voice sounded a whisper.

"He's going to be okay," Sheriff Carpenter said.

"Step aside, everyone," a gruff yet familiar voice said.

I was surprised to see Dr. Hargrove, the man who had served as our family's doctor for as long as I could remember. He retired years ago and had turned his practice over to his son. Dr. Hargrove was an old man now. His hair had turned snow white, and his eyes had a disjointed, rheumy look to them.

"Dr. Hargrove?"

"Don't try to move, Sarah. Your arm is broken and I am waiting for one of those young FBI agents to bring me the supplies I need to set it and splint it. Would someone please tell me what's going on here? Why is the FBI at Bennett House?"

If someone answered him, I didn't hear.

I was still lying on the floor in the foyer, but someone had placed something under my head and had covered me with a blanket. Dozens of men, all wearing the same non-descript suits, milled around the door that led to my father's office. The front door opened and a young man who I had never seen before headed up the stairs, passing another man who was coming down. I was curious about them for a second, until my arm started to throb.

Dr. Hargrove knelt down next to me.

"Look to the right," Dr. Hargrove said. "Now look left." He prodded my neck and shoulders. When he touched my arm, I cried out. The room started to spin. A man that I had never seen before approached the doctor. He held out the well-worn medical bag to Dr. Hargrove.

"Here you go," he said. "I got everything from the office, not that I'm usually a messenger."

"Thank you, young man," Dr. Hargrove said as he took the proffered bag. I had a vague recollection of him saying, "We need to move her to the couch so I can set her arm," then I slipped away.

When I awoke, I found myself situated on the sofa in the library, covered with a blanket, my head resting on a pillow. The fire blazed. Dr. Hargrove stood with his back to me as he packed his medical bag. Zeke sat in the winged chair by the fire. When he saw me looking at him, he came over to me, sitting on a tiny footstool that had been moved close to the sofa. "Did the police arrest her?" I asked.

He shook his head. Before he could say anything, Dr. Hargrove interrupted.

"Don't worry about that," Dr. Hargrove said. He turned to Zeke. "I don't want her moved. She needs complete rest. I'm going to give her something for the pain, and I'll be back to check on her later."

I couldn't bear hypodermic needles, so I looked away while Dr. Hargrove took the glass syringe from the worn leather case and filled it with something. Soon I felt the prick of the needle, the flush of the drugs, and the waves of relief. I fell into a drug-induced sleep and dreamt.

I envisioned Vivian, lying dead on the floor of the foyer. In my misty, drug-induced fugue, I went to her. I bent down, examining her still, peaceful countenance. Vivian in death looked a gentle soul. My father's book lay open on her chest, resting on her heart. I reached out a hand to touch her pale, cold skin. The motion of bending over her body caused my mother's locket, which had been tucked under my shirt, to come loose and swing over her face. Her eyes snapped open. When they met mine, she started laughing, the hysterical cackle of a madwoman. She grabbed the locket from my neck and started to pull on it. I awoke with a start.

"My locket," I cried out, using my good hand to reach for the necklace. The locket was safe around my neck, but I had been dressed in a nightgown and covered with a warm blanket. I wondered who had dressed me, but drifted back to sleep before I could give it much thought.

When I awoke, the morning light which came through the windows warmed my skin. Outside the gulls cried. I had slept for hours. My back had become stiff and painful. I tried to sit up, winced, and lay back down.

"Hello." Zeke must have stayed with me all night, as he had a blanket over his knees and still wore the same clothes he had on yesterday.

"Are you all right?" I knew without sitting up that I was weak and dizzy.

"Just a little queasy."

"How did you know she slipped something into your drink," I said.

"She had her back turned a little too long, and then she had this look in her eye as she watched me lift the glass to my lips. I just knew right here." He touched his hand to his heart, a gesture that reminded me of my mother, that day on the beach.

"Where's Vivian? Did the FBI find anything?"

"Are you thirsty or hungry? Dr. Hargrove said you were to be given water and broth." He helped me to sit up, propped pillows behind my back, and held the glass while I drank some water. He spooned some beef broth into my mouth. It revived me and eased the nausea. He took two pills from a bottle that had been left by the sofa and handed them to me. "You need to take these pain pills, Dr. Hargrove's orders." He held the glass of water to my lips.

"Vivian Mason broke her neck in the fall and died instantly. You got lucky, Sarah, and landed on top of her. When I found you, I saw the banister and the shattered table. You were laying there, your arm—you could have been killed."

"She told me she killed my mother. She had no remorse at all." I shivered. "So cold blooded."

"She's evil," Zeke said.

"Zeke, I need to tell you," I said.

He leaned close to me and touched my forehead. "What?"

"I remember everything. I know who killed Gran, and I know what happened the night Jessica died."

# CHAPTER 19

I thought I said that she couldn't be moved," Dr. Hargrove barked at Zeke. His eyes blazed with fury and his face had become so mottled, I was afraid he was going to have a heart attack.

Zeke and I had taken two adjoining rooms at The Bennett Arms. I had packed in a hurry, only grabbing the few nice pieces of clothing I had, the pictures that Vivian Mason had stolen from my bedroom, and a dozen of my favorite books.

Now, Dr. Hargrove stood in the nicer of the two rooms that Zeke had insisted I take for my own use. He had one gnarled hand resting on the marble mantle, the other pointed at Zeke, who paced back and forth in the front of the window that overlooked the street. We were waiting for Sheriff Carpenter to come, while Zeke kept a vigil on the street below.

"We had a situation, sir," Zeke said. "Sarah was no longer safe at Bennett House. I made a decision—"

"Actually, I made the decision." I interrupted Zeke. "I was able to travel and I am not any worse for it. I don't want to discuss it further. Zeke, if you'll excuse us, I'm ready for Dr. Hargrove's ministrations." I forced a smile and tried to act like my back wasn't hurting and my arm wasn't throbbing.

"I'm going to leave the door ajar.' Zeke made sure the window was secure. He checked the door that led into the hallway for the fourth time, with Dr. Hargrove watching him with a petulant look on his face.

"Would you care to tell me what's going on?"

"I can't, Dr. Hargrove. I'm sorry," I said.

"Well, you can't fool me, young lady. You're in pain. I can tell by the look on your face."

My hotel room faced the west and was filled with afternoon light. It was a charming room, with walls which were painted a warm turquoise blue, a low-beamed ceiling and knotty pine floors covered with white wool rugs. The small fireplace had two chairs before it. The single bed was tucked in a corner. There was a small desk, a bathroom with a huge claw foot tub and plenty of hot water, such a contrast to Bennett House, with its large, cold rooms that were never warm, no matter how bright the fires burned.

"Lay on your side." Dr. Hargrove examined my spine, checked the splint he used to set my broken arm, and took my pulse. "You're a very lucky woman, Miss Bennett. Your stepmother wasn't so fortunate. I've spoken to Sheriff Carpenter, told him that you shouldn't be bothered for another day or two. At some point you will need to speak to him. He will want a statement from you."

I didn't have the heart to tell the good doctor that Sheriff Carpenter was already on his way over here to get a statement from me, not only about Vivian's death, but also about Gran's murder and the night that Jessica fell down the stairs at Bennett House.

"I can give you a shot of morphine for the pain."

"No, thanks, Dr. Hargrove," I said. "If I need one, I'll call."

He grunted, and was gone.

We hadn't heard from my father since he left for New York. We had never been able to reach him at the Algonquin, and the messages we had left so far had gone unanswered. After the doctor left, Zeke came back into the room with Sheriff Carpenter in tow. They sat down in the winged chairs, which we positioned before the fire. I remained standing for the sake of my back.

"I came as soon as Zeke called me," Sheriff Carpenter said. "He said you've remembered the night of Jessica's death, and that it ties in with your grandmother's murder?"

I nodded.

"Why do I think I'm not going to like what she says," he said to Zeke.

"Because it's the worst case scenario, but I believe her. It makes perfect sense," Zeke said.

Sheriff Carpenter leaned back in his chair, crossing his arms over his chest, as if to ward off what I had to tell him.

I told him everything that I remembered about the night my adoptive mother died and finished by telling him how the events of that night twelve months ago had led to Gran's murder.

Sheriff Carpenter didn't speak, didn't say one word for a good five minutes. My back throbbed. I needed to lie down. I looked at the bed with longing. Zeke jumped out of his chair, put his arm around me, and led me to it.

"She's going to lie down. It's her back. She hurt it when she fell." He helped me to lay on top of the counterpane.

"What a remarkable series of events. I can't believe it." The sheriff ran his hand over his mouth, and rubbed his upper lip. "But it makes sense. I could see how someone could be driven—but your story is pure conjecture. There's no hard proof."

"Not now," Zeke said. "There's no proof now, but at least we have something to go on, a place to start."

"I don't want you two doing anything about this without my permission. Do you understand? No heroics, no renegade cowboy, just step back and let the professionals handle this, okay?" Sheriff Carpenter's gaze travelled from Zeke to me and back to Zeke again. He didn't trust us. I didn't blame him.

His arthritic knees cracked as he stood up. "I'm too old for this job," he said under his breath. "Sarah Jane, rest up and get better."

"I will."

Zeke walked the sheriff to the door and stepped out into the hall with him. When he came back into the room, he found me trying to sit up, which was proving difficult with one arm.

"I know how we can prove what happened," I said.

"I think we should wait—" Zeke started to speak but I interrupted him.

"No, his hands are tied, and he's afraid of the consequences. He's not going to do anything." I grabbed the car keys from my nightstand. "We need to go to Bennett House."

# CHAPTER 20

Even though we had been gone for a mere twelve hours, Bennett House looked desolate and deserted when Zeke and I pulled up to the front door.

"You sure you're up to this? You can wait in the car while I—"

"No, I know what we're looking for. I'm going in with you."

We got out of the car and used my key to unlock the front door. Once inside I shivered, glad for my warm sweater. I stood in the foyer, trying to conjure up the memory of Anca's bread baking, our laundry hanging in the kitchen, Jessica's laughter ringing in the drawing room. I couldn't.

When Bennett House was built, there were no banks or safe places to hide money, so my great grandfather had the foresight to install a safe room, which Jessica had shown me years ago. She had regaled me with stories of pirates and faeries and all sorts of creatures that had lived in the cubby hole where my great grandfather kept his gold and silver. Those stories in themselves were treasures, an oral homage to Jessica's talent as a storyteller. I now sought her journals, for in them she had recorded her life, her loves, her losses, and—I hoped—the stories that she hoped to publish one day. But Jessica's dream of becoming a writer got set aside when she married Jack Bennett and they adopted a little girl.

When she discovered what her husband had intended to do, steal the stories that she had written so long ago and claim them as his own, a horrible argument had ensued. In a fit of rage, Jack had pushed Jessica who, in turn, tumbled down the stairs to her death. I had come out of my bedroom into the hall to see what the ruckus was about, had run down the stairs to Jessica, who lay in a heap at the bottom. I cradled her in my arms, and clung to her long after she had taken her last breath. The shock of their argument, Jessica's fall, and her dying in my arms had induced amnesia. Lucky for Jack Bennett, I didn't remember a thing from that night. Until now.

Moving so as not to stress my back, Zeke and I went through the kitchen, past the servant's staircase, and into the room where the washing machine was kept. We went to the corner where the cubby hole was and moved all the detritus which had accumulated over the years in front of the small door. Zeke held the flashlight, while I searched in the dark recesses for the proof of Jack's big lie. There, just as I remembered them, were the journals that belonged to Jessica.

"You were right," Zeke said. "Let me crawl in there and get those."

"Thanks," I said.

He crawled into the cubby hole and handed me the notebooks, one after another.

There were a dozen notebooks all told, bound in leather that was once Kelly green, but which had now faded to a dingy gray. We took all of them to the kitchen, set them on the refectory table.

Zeke got the dishcloth that Anca had hung on the hook—was that just yesterday? It seemed like a lifetime ago. After we cleaned most of the dust and grime off the journals, we set about reading them. The one I chose was written when Jessica was just a child, and although her musings were interesting, the prose in this book was not what I was looking for. Zeke read the journal he had, looking for that one sentence.

I found the story I was looking for in the last journal, the memorable opening line, "Chloe watched her brother drown in a stream…" So the story started, written in Jessica Bennett's beautiful cursive writing. The story was a good one, thus my father's success.

"I have it," I said. We put the rest of the notebooks back, closed the cubbyhole, and were ready to leave Bennett House.

"This house is different," Zeke said. "It's gloomy now."

"I can't shake the feeling that we're being watched," I said. "I know it sounds paranoid."

I walked ahead of Zeke. When we passed through the kitchen, I heard him groan behind me and fall to the floor.

I turned around. Jack stood over Zeke's crumpled form, a pistol in his hand.

I looked down at Zeke. He lay on his side, between Jack and me, with his back toward me. I tried to bend down to check if he was okay, but the pain in my back radiated like white heat up my spine, cascading in flashing stars behind my eyes. How many hits was Zeke going to take for me?

"We know what you did," I said, brandishing the notebook. "You stole her ideas. She didn't like it, didn't agree to you publishing her work under your name. You fought. You pushed her down the stairs."

"I knew it was just a matter of time before you remembered. That's why I had to get you home, so I could keep an eye on you."

"When did Gran discover your little secret?"

"Jessica gave a copy of that story to her mother after she wrote it. Patricia kept it all these years in that stupid box of mementos. She didn't figure it out for a while, but when she did, she was not happy. She told me if I didn't give her daughter the credit she was due for *Arms of the Enemy*, she would go the newspapers. I refused, and she became suspicious of my actions the night Jessica died."

"So you slit her throat?" I should have been scared, but I wasn't. I was angry. Angry that Jessica had to die, that Gran had to die, all because Jack wanted the world to think that the remarkable talent possessed by his wife belonged to him. "Why couldn't you just let Jessica publish the book in her name?"

"Because I was desperate for the money. Jessica didn't know that I had spent the money my father left me. What little money Jessica had was held in trust, and Patricia wouldn't never have let me—us—have it. We had a lifestyle to maintain, and I needed to come up with the money fast. All I did was take credit for it. We could have had a symbiotic relationship. She would ghostwrite the stories for me, and I would have gone on book tours. You know how Jessica didn't like to speak in public. We would have made a good team."

"Lucky for you I developed amnesia," I said.

"Everyone in town knows you're crazy, Sarah. That rumor—started by me, thank you very much—set the stage for my grand plan. You're going to write a confession, before you commit suicide. It will be a sad thing, especially for Zeke, but he'll get over it. Sit at the desk."

I sat down at Anca's desk, the little secretary in the

kitchen that she used to make her grocery lists and plan the menus for our family's meals. Jack took a piece of paper from the top drawer and handed me a pen. He pointed the same gun he used to shoot Zeke's bedroom door at me.

"Now write."

"No. You're going to have to shoot me."

"Heroics don't suit you, Sarah Jane." He pointed the gun at my temple and cocked the hammer.

I picked up the pen and started to write as Jack dictated. I confessed to pushing my mother down the stairs, to murdering Gran, and to my own suicide.

"Put your hands where I can see them. Good. Now get up and walk ahead of me, upstairs to your room."

The cast on my broken arm was too heavy to hold above my head, so I ended up walking in front of Jack with my one arm held to the sky, the other hanging painfully at my side.

Jack poked me in the back with the gun. "I hear you and my wife took quite a fall."

White pain shot through my back, into my arms, to my fingers and toes. "Don't you even care that she's dead?"

"Of course, I care, but there's nothing I can do about that, is there? I'm famous. I'll get another wife. She'll be young and pretty. Wives are replaceable. Reputations are not."

Somehow I managed to get up the stairs. When we

got to my bedroom, he ordered me to sit in the chair in the corner.

"You dressed as Vivian that day on the trail, didn't you? You threw a knife at me. Why?"

"Surely you see how perfect that would have been. No? Well, let me explain. You would be dead, and Vivian could take the blame. She was the perfect scapegoat, but you had to ruin that, didn't you? Although all is not lost. I still may be able to take advantage of her death. At least I'll get the insurance money."

I stood there with my mouth agape, unable to reconcile the deranged lunatic with the man who had so lovingly welcomed me home.

"I said sit down."

When he pushed me into the chair in the corner. I gasped from the pain.

"Don't even think about moving," he said.

As if I could, even if I wanted to. He went in the bathroom. Soon the water gushed into the tub and the room filled with steam.

The pain in my back and my arm became unbearable, and I wished I had taken the morphine that Dr. Hargrove had offered earlier. The room started to move in gentle waves. I faced death, but my pain trumped even that. Jack stood in the doorway between the bathroom and the bedroom where I sat.

"Now, Sarah, you're going to have a nice simple suicide. You're going to get into the nice warm tub, and slit your wrists. It won't hurt. You'll just slip away." He spoke as though we were discussing the weather. "See? Everything will be fine. The American readers are waiting for the next Jack Bennett novel. Unfortunately, I can't give them one. But I do need money."

"Gran's life insurance isn't enough?"

"There's never enough, Sarah Jane," he said.

When I didn't move, he grabbed my good arm. The pain of the sudden movement brought me to my knees, but Jack pulled me up and hauled me into the bathroom. Once inside, he shut the door behind us and locked us in.

"Get in the tub."

"No."

"Just do it," he shouted.

I stepped one leg into the tub.

"Now lie down."

"No." I stepped out of the tub, the water dripping off me and forming a puddle on the tile floor.

Jack and I both jumped when Zeke banged on the door.

"Jack, I know you're in there. The police are here. The house is surrounded. Come out."

"You know I can't do that."

"You know as well as I do that you're not going to harm Sarah. I'm coming in." He started banging on the door, which bowed and heaved and threatened to collapse with every hit of his shoulder.

"Good bye, Sarah," Jack said. He pointed the gun at

me and pulled the trigger. I braced for the pain, for death.

Nothing happened. The gun jammed.

I had backed away from Jack, trying to get as far away from his gun as I could. I didn't see the wrinkled floor rug behind me. When I stepped on it, I slipped and tumbled to the floor. Not wanting to land on my back, I reached toward Jack with my good arm—as if he would hold me up. We both went sprawling into a heap on the floor. Jack dropped the gun and it skidded across the tile floor, coming to rest near me.

It seemed as though I were under water. Everything moved in slow motion, Jack spoke, but I couldn't understand what he said, as his words were muted and distorted by some strange energy that surrounded both of us. The spirit of Grace Kensington appeared. She stood between Jack and me, shimmering in a halo of white light. Her eyes lit on the gun. She picked it up, pointed it, and fired. It didn't jam this time.

Jack's eyes opened in surprise. He fell back against the wall, clutching at the red patch that blossomed on his shoulder. As he slid down onto the floor, the blood seeped through his fingers and onto the tile in crimson rivulets.

Zeke came crashing through the bathroom door and found me sitting on the floor, with the gun in my lap. The spirit of Grace had disappeared.

Zeke took the remaining bullets out of the gun and put them in his pocket, before he tucked the gun away in the waist band of his trousers. He helped me to my feet, finally putting a strong arm around me.

"He was going to kill me. Grace—my—she—it jammed when he tried—when he tried—"

My knees gave way. Zeke held me up. Together we remained standing. Jack sat against the wall, his face white as a newly laundered sheet. In the distance, sirens wailed, their haunting cadence getting louder as they approached the house.

"You called the police?"

"Before we left the hotel."

Soon the police cars arrived, sirens screaming. When the officers who stormed the house saw my father's gunshot wound, they called the ambulance. Soon the house was filled with policemen and medics. The result was melee. Again.

My back throbbed. I had to lean on Zeke as we went downstairs, back once again to the library. This time we both sat on the couch. It wasn't long before Sheriff Carpenter came in to speak to us. He took one look at me and told Zeke to take me back to the hotel. He promised to get a statement from me the next day.

Zeke led me out of Bennett House for the last time. I didn't tell him how the spirit of Grace had saved my life. My connection with my real mother's ghost didn't fit the pattern of the ghost stories one read about in novels and newspapers. Those stories always involved a spirit that has unfinished business, which prevents them from crossing over until things are set right. Grace Kensington knew what Fate had in store for me. Jack intended to kill me, and would have succeeded had the spirit of Grace not intervened. My mother had come to save my life.

When we made it back to the hotel, I kicked off my shoes and, too tired to change into pajamas, got under the covers and fell asleep in my clothes. I slept the rest of the day and all through the night. When I awoke the next morning, Zeke had gone. He left a note in an envelope next to my pillow.

> *Sarah,*
>
> *I got called away and had to catch a plane in the middle of the night. You were sleeping so peacefully that I didn't want to awaken you. I don't know when I will see you again, but I do know that I love you, and the thought of your sweet face and kind eyes will provide me with a glimmer of light as I confront the darkness that awaits me.*
>
> *It would be presumptuous of me to ask you to wait, but I will find you when this is over. If you are happy with another, I won't begrudge you that. God knows you deserve some peace in your life.*
>
> *Be well, my love.*

# CHAPTER 21

Things happened fast after that night. I moved to San Francisco and stayed with Anca and her sister. I helped with the cleaning and the shopping, forcing myself to settle into a routine. Magda, Anca's sister, had the patience of a saint and was teaching me to cook.

My heart had a gaping void where Zeke should have been. I did my best to expunge all thoughts of him. Sometimes I succeeded. At other times, the physical ache of my longing for him would invade my entire being, body and soul. I would cry, wondering what could have been, then force myself to snap out of it.

Jack had suffered a complete breakdown on the day he was arrested. He ranted and raved like a madman. I thought he was faking it. Finally, they put him in a straightjacket, gave him a shot of something that dulled him instantly, and took him away. He was being held in a psychiatric facility, pending his trial for the murder of his mother-in-law and the attempted murder of me. The bitter irony of Jack's commitment to an asylum was not lost on me. There wasn't sufficient proof that he pushed Jessica down the stairs. Hamish managed to keep Jack's plagiarism a secret. His books were flying off the shelves. *Arms of the Enemy* was now in its third printing and had been on the bestseller list for thirty weeks in a row. I tried every day to forget about Jack, Vivian, and my time at Bennett House.

Bennett Cove made the headlines after an FBI sting operation led to the arrest of a dozen spies working for the German American Bund. This group had plans to blow up the Golden Gate Bridge and Union Square, but their efforts were thwarted by J. Edgar Hoover and his dedicated agents. I couldn't help but wonder what role Zeke played in their capture. For a few weeks, Vivian Mason's picture was on the cover of every national newspaper.

Rather than drift along without purpose, I enrolled in Miss Macky's Secretarial College in San Francisco. Grace Kensington left me enough money to live on, provided I was frugal, but I wanted to do my part for the war effort. It was time for me to set out on my own and make my own way in the world. I even made a few friends, women I would study with during the week and go to the museums and art galleries and restaurants with on the weekends. We went to the Top of the Mark and Bimbo's and danced with soldiers to the big band sounds of Stan Kenton, Count Basie, and Duke Ellington. San Francisco was alive. We were alive with it.

My friends all offered to fix me up with their brothers, or friends of friends. I explained that I just lost the love of my life, and since so many young men were dying every day, my story rang true. Soon the invitations stopped coming, which suited me just fine because I knew deep in my heart that Zeke and I would be together again.

❧❧❧

I buried Gran on a cold, gray day in December. I returned to Bennett Cove with Anca to attend the funeral at the little church in town, which was filled to capacity with friends of Gran's that I hadn't seen in years.

After the service, everyone filed out of the church, squeezing my hand, kissing my cheek, and wishing me well. Old friends hugged me, told fond stories of Gran's antics, and expressed their sorrow at the circumstances surrounding her death. No one, not even the children who came to the service, called me Spooky Sarah. No one mentioned Jack Bennett. The graveside service was cathartic. I said my goodbyes to Gran and felt better for it.

Soon we were in the limousine, part of the long train of cars in the funeral procession headed back to Gran's cottage for refreshments.

Mrs. Tolliver and Anca had cleaned the cottage and prepared the food for the luncheon that was a celebration of Gran's memory. Now the two women rode in the limousine with me. Mrs. Tolliver, dressed in her Sunday best, was overwhelmed at the big car.

"This is the finest thing I've ever ridden in," she said, as she ran her fingers over the luxuriant leather seats.

"It's easy to get used to the little luxuries," Anca said.

"You've handled it all well," Mrs. Tolliver said to me, "even the love sickness doesn't show."

Anca nudged Mrs. Tolliver, a silent admonishment for speaking of my pain.

"It has been a bumpy few months." I forced a smile. "But I've a new life now, away from here, away from Bennett Cove."

"That Vivian Mason was no good," Mrs. Tolliver said. "I knew the first time I laid eyes on her that she'd bring trouble."

"And you were right about that." Anca smiled at me. "Now let's speak of better things."

"You'll be fine, Sarah," Mrs. Tolliver said. "Your whole life is ahead of you."

"And what about Zeke? Will I forget about him?"

"You're going to marry him," Mrs. Tolliver said. "You mark my words."

∽∾∽

The memorial luncheon was a success. The champagne flowed, the noise level among the guests got louder and more animated as more alcohol was consumed. And then it was over. Finally, the last guest had left. The last plate had been washed and dried. While Anca put away the silver, I plopped down on the couch in front of the fire.

Soon she came to join me. We sat together, neither one of us speaking for quite some time.

"It is good to move on," Anca said. "We must turn our gaze to what the future holds and be mindful of what is happening around us now."

"I'll be okay," I said.

"I know. You're a good girl."

We both stood up, ready to close Gran's house and walk out the front door for the last time.

"I'll start locking up," Anca said.

"I'm going to walk down to the beach."

"Be careful." Anca unfolded a sheet to place over the couch.

I grabbed one of Gran's heavy coats and headed toward the dunes. On the horizon, I could see a huge aircraft carrier being led by tug boats toward the Golden

Gate Bridge, a crippled vessel being led back to the safety of the Golden Gate for repair.

The waves pounded on the sand. I clutched the locket that hung around my neck and felt close to my mother, to my roots, to the yet unknown story of my birth.

"I miss you," I said out loud.

As my fingers caressed the golden locket, the sun broke through the clouds and a lone sunbeam shone on me. The gulls circled and cried overhead, like angels trumpeting a miracle. As the sun warmed me, the desperate longing I had felt for the mother I would never know slipped away once and for all. I acknowledged the release of this burden with a silent thank you to the heavens. Then the sun slipped back behind the clouds, and I was once again standing in the cold, gray light.

I would never know Grace Kensington, the mother from whom I was separated so long ago, but her spirit would live on in me, forever.

# About the Author

Originally from the San Francisco Bay Area, Terry Lynn Thomas married the love of her life, who promised to buy her a horse if she relocated to Mississippi with him. Now that she has relocated, she has discovered that she can be happy anywhere as long as she has her man, her horse, and time to write. Terry Lynn read Mary Stewart, Victoria Holt, and Daphne Du Maurier as a child. These gothic mysteries captured her imagination, never let go, and influence her writing today. When she is not writing or riding her horse, she visits historical houses and cemeteries, hunting for story ideas.

15916960R00151

Printed in Great Britain
by Amazon